A
HOLE
in the
STORY

ALSO BY KEN KALFUS

2 A.M. in Little America
Coup de Foudre
Equilateral
A Disorder Peculiar to the Country
The Commissariat of Enlightenment
PU-239
Thirst
Christopher Morley's Philadelphia (editor)

A HOLE *in the* STORY

A Novel

KEN KALFUS

MILKWEED EDITIONS

Published 2025 by Milkweed Editions
Printed in Canada
Cover design by Mary Austin Speaker
Author photo by Adachi Pimentel
25 26 27 28 29   5 4 3 2 1
First Edition

Library of Congress Cataloging-in-Publication Data

Names: Kalfus, Ken, author.
Title: A hole in the story : a novel / Ken Kalfus.
Description: First edition. | Minneapolis, Minnesota : Milkweed Editions, 2025. | Summary: "A prescient, high-stakes novel dissecting the ways we tell stories-privately and publicly-amid radical social change"-- Provided by publisher.
Identifiers: LCCN 2024049580 (print) | LCCN 2024049581 (ebook) | ISBN 9781571315755 (hardback ; acid-free paper) | ISBN 9781571315762 (ebook)
Subjects: LCGFT: Novels.
Classification: LCC PS3561.A416524 H65 2025 (print) | LCC PS3561.A416524 (ebook) | DDC 813/.54--dc23/eng/20241105
LC record available at https://lccn.loc.gov/2024049580
LC ebook record available at https://lccn.loc.gov/2024049581

Milkweed Editions is committed to ecological stewardship. We strive to align our book production practices with this principle, and to reduce the impact of our operations in the environment. We are a member of the Green Press Initiative, a nonprofit coalition of publishers, manufacturers, and authors working to protect the world's endangered forests and conserve natural resources. *A Hole in the Story* was printed on acid-free 100% postconsumer-waste paper by Friesens Corporation.

For Inga and Sky

A
HOLE
in the
STORY

ADAM ZWEIG'S PHONE LIT UP. IT WAS A TEXT.

Nice work on the Yang piece! You're so right about the checks.

The message was from Brad Singleton, a reporter for *Axios* with whom he was very casually friendly. They were certainly not friendly enough to compliment each other on their stories. Few of his friends were, really. Most journalists he knew were too competitive to praise each other without being self-conscious: praise could be seen as some kind of concession. And an *acknowledgment* of another reporter's praise could be tendered only with false modesty: yeah, thanks, the story really needed another draft. Yet Adam *had* nailed the problem with monthly cash payments to individuals regardless of need. They were inherently regressive, privatizing resources collected for the common good. But that wasn't why Singleton had texted.

Now a second message arrived.

Btw want to give you a heads-up abt some breaking news call soonest

1

Adam drew his hands back from the keyboard. They had already been stilled. He opened the two texts and reread them.

He looked away from his phone, trying to think what Singleton might want. He refreshed the open tabs for the *Times* and the *Post*. Nothing; or rather it was more shit, breaking news at virtually every refresh. Nothing about Andrew Yang, though. He was still in the race. He seemed to have enough money to make it to Iowa. He was warm and funny and Adam had liked him personally, even with his idiotic "MATH" pin. Adam went to Twitter. Nothing there either, or at least nothing he could imagine Singleton wanting to talk about. He told himself he could call him later, that he should get at least a few more inches into universal health care this morning. But he didn't know what he would write now, and the question raised by Singleton's texts was going unanswered. But he still needed to wait a decent interval before he called back. *Axios* was a second-tier publication, quick with the news, short with analysis. Adam made himself some coffee. He went back to the story and fiddled with the top two grafs.

Then he gave in.

"Adam!" the other reporter exclaimed, as if surprised that he called. "That was some takedown. Yang has no chance anyway, right?"

This was predictably annoying, faithfully reflecting the horse race mindset of these Beltway website hacks, guys who couldn't bother to engage with the candidates' ideas. Adam wasn't going to play, not with his *Guardian* story leading the site and getting social media attention. Any reported comment about Yang's weak electoral prospects would distract from the meaningful elements of the article, which had implications for Democratic social policy beyond the campaign.

"What's up? You had something you wanted to tell me?"

"Yes," Singleton said, pausing. He was fishing for some sign of anticipation. Fuck him. Adam remained silent. Singleton finally spoke. Dropping a register, he pronounced the name, "Max Lieberthol."

Adam said, simply, "Yeah?"

But he quickly refreshed Twitter, just in case. His first thought was that Max had died. He was struck by the first filament of a lightning bolt of grief. There was nothing at the top of his scroll or on the next screen.

"You used to work for Max, right?"

"I still write for them occasionally. But I left the staff a long time ago."

"Yeah, but you were a writer and editor for them in 1999," Singleton confirmed, evidently looking at notes. "So, listen, here's the story. He's been #MeToo'd. He's accused of sexual harassment."

Adam was visited by another lightning bolt, but this one wasn't grief. It was a harbinger of heavy weather.

"That's too bad," Adam said lightly, suppressing any indication that he was being cautious. In the past couple of years a large number of men in journalism and the media, an abundance of men, an overabundance of men, an overflowing superfluity of men, of diverse ages and marital circumstances, had been accused of sexual harassment in the work environment, encompassing various degrees of severity, from rape to attempted rape, to demanding sexual favors for promotion, to groping, to unsolicited back massages, to unexpected kisses— the sexual harassment continuum expanding to include what had seemed to Adam like a vast expanse of male- female interactions. A lewd remark. A collegial meal in a restaurant that, somewhere between the first and second martinis, started to feel like a date. A compliment on an article of clothing. Eyes that rested a moment too long on a figure. A flirtatious remark between a man and a woman of unequal professional status. Almost always, or in fact always, given the male-dominated structure of society, the man was the one with the more advanced professional status. There had been a widely circulated Google spreadsheet, "Shitty Media Men," naming men said to have taken advantage of their positions, mostly in New York. These men and others were losing their jobs and the possibility of getting new ones. It hardly took more than an accusation, every charge being sadly plau- sible, men being what they were. Adam was aware that his casual response could be construed as insufficient. "Very bad," he added, dropping a register himself.

"He's denied it of course."

Adam said, "In sonorous, multi-claused sentences sprinkled with high-flown word choices, I'm sure."

Singleton chuckled. Adam hoped the remark would create some kind of confidence between them, giving the impression of candor.

"Yeah, he issued a statement. I haven't spoken to him directly."

"Good luck with the story," Adam said affably. "I'm not sure how I can help you. It's been so many years since I worked there. But I'll read the piece with interest."

"Thanks," Singleton said, with what sounded like actual gratitude. "The woman's name is Valerie Iovine. Do you remember her?"

Get him off the phone. The main thing now was to think this through. The main thing now was to get Singleton off the phone without sounding like he wanted to get him off the phone. Adam knew how to do this. People he interviewed did it to him all the time.

"Of course I remember her," Adam said with enthusiasm, most of which was genuine. "She was a regular writer for us, on the environment. A contributing writer, I think. I believe she went to a daily in Virginia. Oh damn, it's her?"

"The charge's pretty serious. A direct sexual advance, in his office. She had gone in to discuss a story."

Adam maintained his tone of warm appreciation. "She was a solid reporter. A Harvard graduate, I think. I was sorry to lose track of her."

"Yale. You remember anything about her relationship with Max?"

Adam breathed audibly into the phone to indicate he was thinking. Indeed he was, mostly about how to get Singleton off the phone. Then to consider the implications of Valerie's charges and what might happen next.

He said, "Max was probably as big a pain in the ass with her as he was with everyone else. I don't know about anything personal. I never saw anything. Listen, Brad, thanks for letting me know, but I'm on deadline."

"Me too," Singleton admitted. Adam congratulated himself for the cup of coffee. The reporter said, "I'm not the only one chasing this. But I want to ask you about the office environment."

"C'mon," Adam said sharply. "It was twenty years ago and I worked mostly at home and I really have to go."

Singleton conceded that he needed to file before he got beat. He'd call back for the follow-up. This story was going to have legs.

"Sure, Brad, but I don't know what I can tell you," Adam said. But then, to show that he *wasn't* in an incriminating rush to get off the phone, he added, "Hey, give my best to Helena. Let's go for a drink sometime."

Singleton said OK, pleasantly startled and probably flattered that one of the capital's senior political writers remembered his girlfriend's name. The three of them had run into each other a few months ago at Blackfinn.

They had chatted for no more than a minute. Adam marveled that he had just pulled her name out of his hat.

She had been wearing superskinny white jeans that stopped well short of her low suede boots. He gave himself no points for remembering the turn of her bare ankle.

There was still nothing on Twitter, at least not about Max. Trump was up early this morning at 2:13:40, criticizing the Japanese prime minister for visiting Iran, and then up again at 6:21:50 to praise Mike Flynn, his former national security adviser, who was charged with lying to the FBI about his contacts with the Russian ambassador. The president was still lashing out at the Fake News Media and his FBI director after he was criticized for saying he would accept political dirt about an election opponent from Russia or other foreign governments. "I meet and talk to 'foreign governments' every day." He cited, as examples, the queen of England and the "Prince of Whales." Meanwhile, anticipation was building for the Democrats' first two presidential debates later this month. And press secretary Sarah Huckabee Sanders was stepping down. Someone on Twitter said they wouldn't believe it until they heard her deny it with her own mouth.

Damn. Valerie Iovine. *Damn.*

Adam had watched Valerie go into Max's private office and shut the door that afternoon twenty years earlier. He was technically the first so-called outcry witness.

When Valerie was at the magazine's offices, Adam had always been aware of her presence, keenly sensitive to whatever she was doing in her cubicle three cubicles back, her telephone interviews, the tap of her keyboard, her trips to the coffee station, *pouring* the coffee, her usual shuffle-step. If he turned his head he could watch her return to her desk.

He was her closest friend at the *Next Deal*. She wasn't on staff but she was an increasingly valued writer. They talked out each other's stories and, on the days when they were both there, they went to lunch together, usually at Le Pain Quotidien or Full Kee. Depending on their assignment cycles, they sometimes planned which days they'd come in. She desperately hoped to get on staff. She needed health insurance, even if it was the magazine's crappy bare-bones plan.

She was in Max's office for a while. She had already shown Adam a draft of the global warming piece. Adam thought it was excellent—she had interviewed scientists about potential anti-warming measures—though he knew Max would find a hole. Max always found a hole in your reporting or in your argument. He was never reticent or diplomatic or not triumphant about pointing it out either. And it would be a real hole, a tangible hole. How could you have possibly missed it? From his cubicle, if he rolled his chair a few inches to the left, Adam had a clear view of Max's walnut-paneled door. Another few minutes passed before it opened, forcefully.

He saw the change at once, though not every colleague would have paid enough attention to notice. The change was located most pronouncedly in a dark line above Valerie's brow, all the way across her forehead. It wasn't unusual for a writer to come out of Max's office in some state of crestfallenness. But Adam saw that Valerie's firm, fine-featured face had crumpled. Her eyes were wide. She was on the brink of tears; no, a tear had already gone over the brink, spilling down the left side. Her cheeks were flushed. She strode quickly from the door, no shuffle-step now, back straight, looking directly ahead.

She was headed for the women's restroom, which was located outside the door to the magazine, near the elevators.

Adam could have waited for Valerie to come back and checked on her at her cubicle. The impulse to follow her now, to be there with her at that very moment, was a mysterious one, or it was at least difficult to articulate. He resisted the urge for several minutes, asking himself why he was resisting it. This was difficult to articulate too.

He didn't enter the restroom of course, but he waited outside, down the hall, so he wouldn't surprise her or draw interest from anyone else using the restroom. He would later reflect on these few minutes and try to recall what he had already guessed.

When she came out, she was still not entirely composed, but she had washed her face. As usual, she hadn't applied lipstick or makeup, and her complexion now looked especially raw. She didn't seem surprised to find him waiting for her. He held her eyes as she approached. Something wounded was in them.

"You OK?"

"I'm getting my things and going home."

"Walk you out?"

They rode down the elevator in silence, just the two of them, each watching the floor indicator lights, as if concerned the elevator might lose its way. He knew she was barely aware of his presence. Something was moving through her, back and forth, relentlessly. She might have been in tears again, but he didn't look. They didn't speak as they exited into the lobby of the building, which housed law offices and several obscure federal agencies. Adam and Valerie were two journalists, he in Dockers, she in loose cotton slacks, passing through a midcentury gray marble concourse of thick-bodied white men in business suits and black oxfords. Adam always felt out of place there, in a youngish, sophisticated, freethinking, and thoroughly superior kind of way.

"The story's going to be great," he said once they reached the sidewalk on G Street, though he knew the story wasn't the cause of her upset. She was a pro. She could take a tough edit, even one of Max's fucking blow-up-the-total-premise-of-an-article-we've-already-agreed-on edits. Adam added, "Based on what I read. And everything you told me."

They reached Metro Center. They stood at the top near the escalators. The Metro pit always made him think of something you could fall into and never hit bottom. The early spring day had turned cold. Adam felt it keenly through his Gap button-down. He should have brought his coat, but he had feared that if he went back for it Valerie wouldn't have waited.

"Call me later?" he suggested.

Valerie turned to face him. Yes, those were tears in her eyes again. She said, "He made a pass."

Adam acted surprised. To this day he still wasn't sure how surprised he'd really been. He would have to go back and follow the thread of his intuition. He knew of course that she was referring to Max.

"Shit," he said then. "I'm sorry. What a schmuck."

"We were going over the story. He had some comments. The piece needs work. Then he put down the pages, stared at me, and sighed. One of his big, humongous sighs that are meant to express that he's thinking big, humongous thoughts. Then he said he can't get me out of his head. He said I'm all he thinks about, from lights on to lights out, but his nights are the worst. He lies awake thinking of the day's every encounter, every glimpse. He said what has stirred him is not only my singular presence and my critical smarts and my heterodox sense of humor and the way I brighten the office whenever I come in, but, yes, let's not forget it, my *essential physicality*. That's what he said. He said I was beautiful. He said I was sexy. He wanted to know whether I was in a relationship."

Adam puffed up his cheeks and blew through them. "Max."

"I was stunned. I didn't know what to say."

"What could you say?"

"I just stammered. I mumbled yes I was, but I don't think he heard me, the way he was staring. I just lost it."

"That's OK."

Her tone went flat, as if she were reporting a clinical diagnosis. "He said my breasts were lovely."

Adam made a quick calculation. With some women friends, like the perpetually ribald Charlotte Skinner who covered the White House for the magazine, or even his wife at some more carefree time in their lives together, this declaration might have called for some tension-easing raillery. Like: they are! It might have been funny, with the right delivery. But Valerie wasn't like that. She wasn't sassy or flirtatious and she didn't smile at allusion. Often the youngest person in the office, and technically a freelancer, she wouldn't allow herself a lapse in professional decorum. And whatever closeness she shared with Adam, they had never made jokes about anything sexual. And she was now deeply upset. Maybe about something more than Max.

"I'm sorry," he repeated. "You have a right to be angry. I'm angry too."

She didn't look angry. She looked bewildered. She looked dismayed. She looked stricken.

He very tentatively reached over and brought her to him, the insides of his forearms on her shoulders. She fell into the embrace. This was not what he'd expected at all, he thought later. She moved in and held him closely, making a warm, snug fit with the contours of his body. The sides of their heads touched. She had left open her light denim jacket. She remained pressed against him while travelers rushed by on their way to the escalators. Now he felt through his shirt a shudder of emotional release. The tremor reverberated through his own body. It would echo there the rest of the day. When she pulled away, he was cold again.

Adam said, "I'm not sure I would use the word 'heterodox' to describe your sense of humor. I mean, really? 'Slightly offbeat,' perhaps."

"Let's talk later," she said. "I have to get home and be by myself. I have to finish the fucking story too. He wants it for this issue."

THE FIRST TWEETS were now starting to appear on Adam's feed, linking to an article in *Politico*. Valerie had obviously gone to several news outlets, though *Politico* didn't say so. Singleton's story followed shortly afterward. That sucker got beat after all. Both pieces were brief and written fairly straight, detailing how Max had propositioned Valerie when she was a twenty-six-year-old freelance reporter. They both included Max's comment about Valerie's "lovely" breasts. The *Politico* article, while acknowledging the *Next Deal*'s strong progressive record on women's issues, repeated her charge that Max had promoted within the office a "culture of sexual intimidation." Adam winced at that. The touch on his nerve lingered. Both articles reported verbatim Max's polished, unyielding denial. There was a picture of him. There was none of Valerie. There was also, Adam saw, no third-party support for her claim.

Adam's Twitter feed was predominantly political. He did his due diligence by following commentators left and right, though the algorithm knew which he preferred. The liberal-oriented tweets were now almost gleeful, Max having become an old-time establishment figure. "Another one bites the dust!" already had 314 likes; no, 317; no, 323. Max had made enemies along the way, many of them fast-tweeting journalists. And in Adam's cohort, sexual harassment was unforgivable, no matter how long ago it had taken place. He read expressions of compassion for Valerie, of course, some heartfelt, some of them—by men, Adam observed—blatant virtue signaling. "As a man and a strong progressive, I'm deeply ashamed . . ." etc. Several tortured witticisms were constructed around the magazine's name.

Other jokes were built on Max's name and some of these, apparently from the other end of the spectrum—but who knew?—were inescapably anti-Semitic. Some comments about Valerie were misogynistic, with a few anti-Italian slurs thrown in for fun. More than one troll wanted to know exactly how lovely Valerie's breasts were anyway. Somebody, referring to the magazine's office culture, put up the poster from *La Dolce Vita*, Marcello Mastroianni leering at a prodigiously stacked Anita Ekberg in a low-cut evening dress, which Adam feared was meme-worthy.

Adam was relieved that he had managed to remain unquoted in Singleton's piece, though he knew that his absence from the news cycle wouldn't last long. He was one of several former staff writers who had gone on to prominence, at least in the small but over-oxygenated fish tank of political journalism. He appeared on MSNBC from time to time and was about to appear more frequently as a regular commentator. If Singleton had thought to call him, so would another reporter.

He didn't like or retweet any posts. He was going to stay off social media the rest of the day, or at least as long as possible.

WELL, WHAT *had* the office environment been like?

Adam thought back two decades, nearly in a reverie. It was a pleasing reverie, if you didn't think about the gathering shitstorm.

Mostly the *Next Deal* had been a fun place, staffed by a dozen ambitious young men and women, every one of them proud that they had made it to the nation's capital. They were sociable young people, opinion-ated, well-traveled, earnest, and quick with a joke. The open-plan office had often seemed like the venue for a single continual party, even in the absence of alcohol. If you were between callbacks or stuck on a sentence,

you could always rise from your desk and find someone
with whom to chat, usually about politics or sports or
new films. Or you could just say hello and return to your
desk, where the sentence was still waiting for you.

The alcohol was never missed. The party could
turn raucous without it, especially when a scandal broke.
Gennifer Flowers and Paula Jones. Travelgate and Vince
Foster. The Redskins owner's errant Bolivian-born wife,
who was forty years younger than him. Bob Packwood's
diaries. John Wayne Bobbitt's penis. It was discovered
that felon and four-term mayor Marion Barry's endur-
ing statement of moral principle could be employed
in almost any office situation: "Bitch set me up." The
cries and laughs would approach an uproar. Nothing
was sacred to the young journalists, except of course
journalism itself. Max would come out of his office and
glower. That would bring it down just a notch.

A boy-girl undercurrent was usually palpable within
the course of the festivities, as it was in every newsroom
in which Adam had ever worked, going back to the *Daily
Princetonian*. Single men and women were inclined to
flirt, sometimes vigorously. They dated, too, and last-
ing romantic liaisons often emerged from the magazine
and other newsrooms around the capital, the journalists
eventually proving to be more comfortable with each
other than they were with anyone else. Adam was nearly
forty at the time and married (to a non-journalist, a lawyer), so he wasn't doing any courting, but he never shied

away from frank appreciation of the pretty young women with whom he had collegial relationships.

A sexual *over*current ran through the office as well, a powerful charge of innuendo and often something more explicit than that. The language could be graphic and coarse. The staff felt free to make observations about the physical appearances of assorted politicians, male and female, political operatives, reporters for other publications, and celebrities—rating them for fuckability—and they would from time to time trade across the aisle detailed reports about their own sexual circumstances. From within Adam's cubicle, it sounded like a friendly, comic exercise in competitive raunch.

A new DHL guy brought in some packages, leaving them at the front desk. Max's executive secretary signed for them. As he left, possibly not quite out of earshot, and in fact not out of earshot at all, Skinner muttered, "Nice ass."

Even Adam had observed that the broad-shouldered, crew-cut young man filled out his bright red-and-yellow uniform smartly.

Kathryn McClanahan, over in layout, whispered across the aisle, "Way too young for you."

That may have been audible too.

Skinner was nearly Adam's age. She replied, mock-sultry, "I say, if you bring a bat, let's play ball."

Their younger male colleagues dished out their own crude, comic remarks, often with abandon. Adam tried to stay above the fray without looking like a prude.

Max was older than everyone on his staff, more than
ten years older than Adam, and he kept to his private
office most of the day. He didn't partake in the banter,
but he could be friendly and garrulous and when he
was in the right mood his warmth radiated to every
corner of the office. He came out and checked up on
how people's work was going. He gossiped about the
latest political or media stories and, if it was relevant
to something happening now, he may have reflected on
former political campaigns he had covered. He spoke,
too, about the war in Vietnam. After getting a military
deferment, he had gone to Saigon to cover it freelance.
It was from there that he was hired by the *Sun-Times*
and sent to Washington.

Even as a young reporter, Max must have shown the
same wit and charisma that he brought to the magazine
as editor, and for which he continued to be famous. In
J-schools around the nation, young men and women
studied his career and current work. They embarked on
multiyear campaigns to make themselves known to him.
Those he hired were among the freshest journalistic
minds of their generation. He wrote the magazine's lead
editorial for every issue, employing an almost baroque
style and an erudition that might encompass German
romanticism, English common law, and the Upanishads.
From time to time he contributed to what was called the
back of the book, the arts section, where he commented
on new architecture and contemporary poetry. When

occasion called for it, when he thought the staff might need it, he could also pass through the office singing a few lines from a Broadway show tune, doing a little two-step by the coffee station. Work in the office would stop for these performances.

Max was especially attentive to his women reporters. As a group, the young women he hired were terrific writers, whether they were plucked from graduate school, city desks, state houses, or, in a few cases, war zones. The women were also strikingly attractive, very often of a type: slim, sharp-featured, and either Jewish or of some Mediterranean ethnicity. They were Ivy League, too, of course, like the men on the staff. Max worked with them on their stories line by line. He made suggestions about the kinds of stories and areas of expertise that would most likely further their careers. Many were destined for senior, better-paying positions at major news organizations.

Adam hadn't thought it unusual for his women colleagues to be attractive. Most young professional women were good-looking in one way or another, and often in several pleasing ways, and they flooded the streets of downtown Washington, if not in as great a number as they did in New York. They wore flattering clothes and makeup and they styled their hair. Studies showed, he knew vaguely, the professional advantages prettier women held over plainer women in hiring and in advancement, even while facing discrimination as women. Taller men did better than men of medium height too. Like most people, Adam always accepted this situation as a matter of course. He didn't think it unjust that he had worked harder to get to where he was than a taller man would have.

Photo editors, including Larissa Karapetyan at their own magazine, always showed a preference for using a picture of an attractive woman, even if she was less central to the story. A story built around an attractive woman politician or woman thinker was likely to make the cover, or was even the reason for it being in the magazine in the first place. A woman on the cover was presumed to help newsstand sales, even for an exceedingly wonky current affairs periodical. The *Next Deal*'s (few) advertisements for commercial products like new automobiles always featured glamorous women models, of course.

Adam's wife was an attractive woman, probably too comely to be working as an ACLU death penalty lawyer, in a modestly appointed office where she was surrounded by male lawyers of limited height.

In the twenty years since the incident with Valerie, Max Lieberthol had finally married. The wife was also pretty, dark-haired, and delicately featured, a former culture reporter for the *Next Deal* who had joined the staff sometime after Adam left. She was much younger than Max, younger than Adam, and she had gone on to write a biography of Hannah Arendt that was nominated for a National Book Award. The *Times* review featured

a picture of the author, not Hannah Arendt. As far as
Adam knew, Max was a good husband. They had a ten-
or eleven-year-old girl on whom he doted. The girl loved
Broadway show tunes too.

"Another one bites the dust!" was up to 1.7K. There
was also a hashtag, *#Lieberlover*, the redundancy a particular species of Twitter humor. Nothing was up yet on
the *Times* or the *Post*; it was a busy news day in a busy
news week/month/year/epoch. Adam hadn't been called
again, but he hadn't made any progress on his story since
the call from Singleton. Nor had he done anything with
the contract he was supposed to return to Nuri Gelman
at the network. He was still trying to figure out how to
get more money out of her.

Max wasn't going to resign over the *Politico* story
or some Twitter bullshit, no matter how loud it came in
on Adam's feed or the feeds of other Washington journalists. He would ignore the tweets or be truly unaware
of them. He had fought battles bigger than anything on
Twitter: with Bill Clinton (after demanding his resignation), with the Reagan Justice Department (a subpoena
over an Iran-Contra source), and with Nixon (who had
given him a shout-out on the tapes).

His name could hardly be separated from the magazine, which he had founded thirty-five years ago. A
couple of outside investors had provided the money,
but Max was the one who gave the magazine its identity,

shaping it around his ideologies, his enthusiasms, and his personal quarrels. The magazine's voice was his. His grand cadences sounded through every leg of type, no matter which of his writers had composed it. Even Adam, even when writing for other publications, often sounded like Max. Max's peculiar word preferences and fancy locutions made it into Adam's copy and the pieces written by other former colleagues all over the capital. Even Obama had sometimes sounded like Max, despite being pissed off at him half the time.

The original money guys were long gone, though they still allowed themselves to be celebrated for their places in the magazine's origin story. The influential but chronically undersubscribed publication had passed through several hands over the decades, repeatedly being bailed out by rich men, often robber baron heirs, sometimes non-publishing entrepreneurs, always vaguely liberal, who nevertheless had nothing to do with the magazine's editorial direction. As a condition of ownership, they were told to fuck off.

The latest owners were some finance dudes for whom the magazine's operating budget was just one of several recherché tax write-offs. They had started out in California but had moved the firm to the island of Jamaica, even though the Commonwealth nation wasn't especially hospitable to the finance industry. They weren't involved with the magazine's day-to-day and they never showed their faces in Washington, not even being forwarded the invitations to the cocktail parties they were entitled to attend. Max called them once a year to tell them how much of a shortfall they had to make up.

Adam didn't know to what extent they cared about their investment, but it was entirely tied up in Max's stewardship of the *Next Deal*: his name, his writing style, and his intellect. No Max, no magazine. This syllogism made Adam realize, with a start, that *he* had a significant investment in the magazine, even though he rarely wrote for it these days. If the magazine folded, a rigorously pragmatic, farseeing, big-picture, contrarian voice would be lost to American progressive thought, just when the nation needed it the most. Adam depended on the magazine coming to his house every two weeks—he studied the table of contents as soon as he removed the issue from his mailbox—but Max's departure would be a disaster far beyond the personal.

IT HAD BEEN TRUE, Valerie Iovine did have lovely breasts. Adam had always been aware of them. He assumed everyone in the office, women and men, had been aware too. The breasts floated almost weightless beneath her light, pastel-colored shirts and sweaters, often poking out skyward whether or not she was wearing a bra that day, a question in which he took a keen interest. They were small breasts, but he had guessed they were high and spherical. When she wore tight blouses they showed like . . . like some fruit smaller than most melons, but with the same perfect roundness. She'd pass his desk and he'd glance at her narrow, straight back to look for the telltale strap.

This was wrong, wrong, wrong, of course, and he had been ashamed of his steady male gaze at the time, if not as mortified or as close to mortified as he was now in recollection, even if the memory also brought him pleasure. In all his years as a man and a boy before then, and in all the years since, he had never really learned the proper attitude to assume in observing the physical form of a woman with whom he wasn't intimate. He knew he was not to study it too long or too carefully or with any suggestion of sexual appetite. You could look at her face and figure in a *certain* appreciative way; not *other* appreciative ways. All these years being a man, and a man not unfamiliar with feminist thought, and he still wasn't sure how to resolve what seemed, perhaps incorrectly, like an unresolvable tension.

And then, on a day that would forever blaze in his memory, before the thing with Max, before the thing with *him*, Valerie came to his cubicle wearing a white button-down blouse, its top two buttons open. She wanted to show him the layout on her story, unhappy about a picture. Standing over his left shoulder, she laid the page proof on his desk. He saw at once that the photo of the senior senator from New York was wrongly scaled, too big for the page, and poorly shot as well. What was Larissa thinking? Valerie leaned over to show him a bad line break at the bottom of the second column of type. He turned, the third button slipped from its mooring, and he saw that this wasn't a day she was wearing a bra. Her creamy left breast was fully visible and he saw precisely how globular it was, and compact, rising away from the inside of the open shirt, with a freckle near the aureole, and the pinkish aureole, and the much darker, slightly elevated nipple. He drank in the extended moment and then abruptly turned away to compensate for the moment, though it was clear to both of them that he had deliberately taken that moment-extension, that he had seen her left breast. She stood upright and the shirt straightened itself. He could still see the nipple through the shirt, or it might have been a ghost image burned into his retina. He directed his attention to the photo on the page. He said, "Right, let's ask them to use a vertical."

"Moynihan coming off the train?"

He nodded, not looking up, hoping that she wouldn't see how red in the face he probably was, or at least how red his ears were. They burned. Adam was an easy blusher.

She left to talk to the layout desk and he continued to meditate on what he had just seen. In terms of the male gaze, in terms of women-viewing, an enterprise that was an integral, if casual, part of Adam's life, this was like hitting the jackpot. Most women wore bras these days. You could spend years looking down their shirts without seeing a naked breast. He thoughtfully reviewed what he had seen of Valerie's and compared them to others he knew and had known, including his wife's. Those, too, when they were unclothed, were still an object of study, every time.

His awareness of Valerie's breasts and other womanly parts may have been heightened after that. She continued to move through the office coolly, from cubicle to coffee station to photo editor to layout desk. On the days when her nipples were visible through her shirt, he tracked their positions. He presumed all the men in the office did. Did she know that? Did she care? To what extent did she wish them to be seen? Even without makeup, even dressed down in jeans, Valerie was attentive to her appearance. And she knew there was such a thing as the male gaze, and how dehumanizing it was. Adam knew it too.

He also knew, at the time twenty years ago, which was not so far in the past, that it had been wildly inappropriate for her editor to make a romantic advance in her direction. And of course it was boorish for him to speak of her breasts, and not really comprehensible. Max was a sophisticated man, out in the world. He was a fixture of liberal political society. You'd think he'd know how to behave around women, especially women who worked for him—especially now, a few months after the dismaying spectacle of Clinton's impeachment. It was said that the Monica Lewinsky scandal had reset the norms of office male-female relations. And what was the purpose of Max's declaration? Did he think, after his frantic confession of desire, that the compliment to her breasts would be *seductive*?

The offense may have been compounded by Max's advanced age and girth, which presumably took him off the romantic market, especially for women of Valerie's age, more than twenty years younger. Though maybe he wasn't off the market. Even the most self-possessed, progressive, feminist women were attracted to men of accomplishment and power, in the media as well as in politics. You encountered these couples at parties, at restaurants, at parent-teacher nights. This mysterious phenomenon was observed time and again, and not only in the nation's capital.

VALERIE CALLED ADAM the evening after the incident with Max. He took the call in his home office. The family had each retreated to their own places, Jason in his bedroom, locked inside an AOL chat room, Luann at the dining room table, where she had spread out death penalty briefs every night for the past two weeks. Valerie asked how the family was, how the rest of the day had gone, and if he had a moment to talk. She was immediately apologetic.

"I made too big a deal of it."

"Not at all," he insisted.

"I'm a big girl," she said. "I've faced this before, I can handle it. I'm furious with myself. I used to cover the Philly cops. I heard plenty. This is nothing."

She paused but he didn't think she was waiting for his response. She was collecting herself, thinking about what she wanted to say. How much.

He replied, "You should expect more from your editor."

She said, more softly, "Adam, I'm just a little shaky these days. A little fragile. And I went into Max's office and I was blindsided."

"I bet you were."

"It's coming at a tough moment."

Adam had a premonition, just as he did when he saw her leave Max's office. He didn't want to show he was anticipating anything, so he didn't ask whether she had told her boyfriend yet.

He said instead, a little inanely, "If you're worried about your story . . ."

She told him, "I don't think Josef and I are really together anymore. I'm not sure. Something cooled there. I tried to ask him what was going on. He said nothing was wrong, vehemently, angrily. So I wasn't exactly reassured. We haven't seen each other in two weeks. We were planning to go to Wolf Trap on Sunday, for a Del McCoury show. I don't think that's happening."

Adam knew Josef, or at least they had met a few times. He was a tall, rangy Czech with an anachronistically bushy mustache and sideburns, a genetics scientist at George Washington. He had arrived in America five years earlier with a passion for bluegrass, surprised to discover that it wasn't the nation's dominant popular music.

Adam and Luann had once gone out to dinner with them. The company hadn't really gelled. Adam and Valerie struggled to avoid exchanging Washington media gossip. Luann liked Valerie, but neither she nor Adam were able to carry on a conversation with Josef, even though he initially seemed friendly enough. When Adam asked him what he was working on, the boyfriend said, "You wouldn't understand." Adam was so offended he laughed. Then, as if Josef were the subject of an interview, Adam continued to interrogate him about his research, in the face of the young man's increasing annoyance. Adam pressed on. As a matter of principle, he believed in the Enlightenment ideal that all things could be made understandable to all people of at least standard intelligence, and that every scientist or academic, no matter how esoteric his field, should be able to explain his work to the layman in two or three sentences, especially if the work was in any way funded by society. Adam failed to get three enlightening sentences out of the guy. Valerie couldn't explain Josef's work either. "He does what he does, and I do what I do," she told Adam later, apparently not sharing her friend's misgivings about the relationship.

"Maybe it's just a lull?" he said now. "Something going on with him?"

"When Max asked if I was in a relationship . . . it was like he *knew*. Like the whole *world* knew. And I didn't."

"Max knows nada. He doesn't know about Josef in the first place."

"Like people are doubtful about my ability to have a relationship at all. Like everyone sees something wrong with me that I can't see. Or I *can* see but won't admit."

"Now you're talking crazy, Valerie. You're smart, accomplished, and at least a little bit charming, on a good day. You've had boyfriends before. You'll meet someone else. Don't go off the deep end on me."

"My first thought, before he even spoke about my breasts, was to wonder how I had fucked up, how I had brought this on. I was already wondering how I had fucked up with Josef and with all the other guys in the past. My whole life of getting involved with men seems like one misunderstanding after another. I admire Max! I'm amazed that I'm writing for him. I've tried to respond to his support and his warmth, but I've never felt that way toward him. Have I been sending him signals that I'm interested? What signals? I thought I was being normally friendly. Was it my clothes?"

"There's nothing wrong with your clothes," Adam said hurriedly, worried that she would stop wearing tight blouses. "Look, there's a basic fact underlying everything in human existence. That fact is this: men are idiots."

She blurted, "You're not an idiot!"

"As big as they come," he snapped, yet he was warmed by her endorsement. "Really, I'm sorry this happened and maybe the thing with Josef is just a bump in the road. In any case, I'm pretty confident you're going to be all right."

"Thank you, Adam," she said with feeling.

"You finish your story?"

"I've been just too upset."

"Listen," Adam said. "If you want to say fuck it, that's OK. But the issue closes tomorrow."

"I know. I'll rewrite it tonight. But I have to discuss Max's comments. The ones not about my breasts. He wants me to move up carbon sequestration. That messes up the section after the nut. Can you look at it? And he says it's already a thousand words too long."

She sent him the latest draft and they spent nearly another hour on the phone, talking almost entirely about the story, but their personal exchange continued on another track parallel to their consideration of global warming. It was made evident in the gentle tones of voice they used with each other, the tact that accompanied his writing suggestions, the readiness with which she received them, his encouragement, her vulnerability, and the closeness with which they moved together toward completing the article. Putting sequestration after the introductory nut paragraph was a good idea. Max was right again. By the time Adam hung up, it was well past the household's usual bedtime. Jason had to be separated from his computer. Adam found his wife in the dining room in the same position that he had left her.

Luann was hunched over her papers and turned only when Adam called her name. She blinked as if she were just regaining her sight, having just come back from a journey underground, which in a sense she had. Her face was drained of color, except that her deep-set eyes were rimmed red. They appeared even more deep-set this late into the night. Her long wavy hair spilled from her head like a waterfall. Her features were held in a spasm of anger and pain and Adam thought, not for the first time, of a vengeful goddess, a Fury in all her power and beauty.

"The police," she spat. "The fucking, goddamn, criminal, incompetent, *criminally incompetent*, mother-fucking police."

THE SKIES ABOVE eastern Oklahoma were clear the evening of March 5, 1983, and the moon was up, just past full. Hobart Stubbs, a twenty-two-year-old unemployed laborer, parked his nine-year-old avocado-green Pinto in front of the Stop & Shop convenience store on Route 11 in the Northside section of Tulsa. He left the car unlocked. He pulled a red-and-white Sooners bandanna over his face and entered the store, where the owner, Vernon Hummel, was behind the counter putting some things away. This was Stubbs's second visit of the afternoon. He had come to the store around three o'clock and purchased a forty-ounce Mickey's. He was returning now with a Glock 17 that he had borrowed from a friend who would later testify that he had no idea what it would be used for, only that Stubbs said he needed "protection."

The robbery had been conceived that afternoon, its urgency had been realized as he descended deeper into the bottle of malt liquor, and its apparent practicality was made evident the moment his friend showed off the Glock. Before he left home, standing in front of a mirror, he had practiced with the bandanna and the gun.

Focused on the crime he was determined to accomplish, his first robbery, Stubbs wasn't immediately aware that Hummel wasn't alone. The store owner had been alone earlier in the day and every previous time Stubbs had come there. Stubbs swung open the door, raised the gun, and shouted for him to empty the cash register. He had meant to say "hands up" first. Now Stubbs realized that a woman and a girl were in the store too. They were Hummel's wife, Astra, and their fourteen-year-old daughter, Theodora, who were helping him close the store. Stubbs was taken aback. He was anxious. Their presence in the store, their actual existence, had never been part of the plan.

Hummel raised his hands anyway. It wasn't like he hadn't been robbed before. Astra and Theodora raised their hands too. Stubbs was hardly able to speak, but he managed to wave his gun at the woman and the girl to indicate that they should move in the direction of the refrigerator case.

He came around the counter, where Vernon Hummel was still at the register. Stubbs had planned to tell him to open it, asshole, but he still couldn't get the words out. He pointed the gun at the machine. Astra and Theodora were just at the edge of his vision, which was partially blocked by the bandanna.

Hummel pressed the NCR 6000's Cash button. At that moment, as the drawer slid open, Stubbs saw that the shop owner kept a pistol on a shelf beneath the machine. Panicked by the gun and also by the woman and the girl behind him and additionally by the abrasive sound of the drawer's opening, the clanging and crashing of the change coins as they shifted in the drawer, as well as by the machine's mechanical bell, and also by the suddenness with which the drawer obscured the location of the pistol, Stubbs fired a single shot into Hummel's chest. Theodora cried out and, hardly turning, Stubbs shot her, too, killing her at once. Hummel slumped to the floor, still alive.

Stubbs removed $82.46 from the drawer, his hands shaking. Astra whimpered, moving to embrace her daughter's lifeless body. As Stubbs ran toward the door, he shot twice. He hit Astra once in the shoulder.

Adam was the same age as Hobart Stubbs. He could almost figure out what he and Luann had been doing that night in 1983, a Saturday, during the second semester of his senior year. Luann had been a junior. She had probably been studying at Firestone, head down in a book. He would have been sitting across the table intently reading *The Power Broker*, as he had done all that winter in neglect of his coursework, trying to learn from Robert Caro's every move. They would have gone to Adam's off-campus apartment afterward. They would have made love.

About ten minutes after Stubbs left the store, once the severely wounded Astra Hummel was able to stand,

she went to the phone next to the register and called
the police, smearing the phone with her own blood and
her daughter's.

The dispatcher didn't fully comprehend what Astra
was saying. He couldn't make out her garbled words'
import. The cops took their time, arriving thirty-eight
minutes later. Vernon was dead by then. The officers
and the medics made a botch of the crime scene investigation, removing Vernon's and Theodora's bodies
before taking a full set of pictures. They didn't immediately dust for prints. Stubbs was arrested only because
the police found him in his car in an empty parking
lot, the motor left on, the bandanna under his chin, the
gun in the passenger's seat. He was in a kind of stupor,
frightened and amazed by what he had done.

The Tulsa County public defenders showed hardly
more competence than either Stubbs or the police,
vainly trying to secure a plea deal before their own investigation of the case was complete. Conviction was swift
and so was the decision to impose the death penalty, but
challenges to the sentence, even with the local lawyers'
worst efforts, would simmer for years.

Once the ACLU became involved, Luann's office
had quickly identified the most obvious problems with
the case. Astra Hummel's identification of the killer
was uncertain. The evidence's chain of custody had
been compromised by poor recordkeeping. The medical examiner extracted bullets from the victims' bodies

and then *lost them*. None of these issues had been raised more than minimally by the state PDs.

Even by Oklahoma's standards of criminal justice, the trial conduct had been appalling. Luann came home every night with the transcripts, key passages of which she read to Adam and Jason at dinner, dramatizing the statements of the witnesses, the lawyers, and the judge. While Adam couldn't follow every twist and turn of the trial, or understand every legal malfeasance that Luann thought was heart-stoppingly self-evident, he saw the case's weaknesses. Twelve-year-old Jason saw them too.

Luann had been uncovering further police misconduct. They had lied to Stubbs, telling him that the killings were witnessed by someone on the road outside the shop. The friend's statement about the gun was coerced. Night after night, working at the dining room table, Luann traced the ramifications of the original misconduct.

"An Okie horror show," she said.

Not that it was likely that the conviction could be reversed. The cops had found Stubbs with the weapon. Several five- and ten-dollar bills in his wallet were stained with Vernon's blood. He confessed. But the local PDs had seemed confused and listless during the subsequent penalty hearings, when they were allowed to make arguments to save his life. They failed to stress that Stubbs had not intended to kill Vernon when he entered the shop. Nor did they argue that Vernon would have lived if the police had been more responsive. As for Theodora: that unlucky shot was a startle response to her cry. Also, Stubbs had been intoxicated. And in his car, even before his arrest, he had been overcome by strong emotions that included grief and remorse.

Every several weeks Luann flew to Tulsa, rented a car, drove two hours to the city of McAlester, and checked in at the Holiday Inn. It was a ten-minute drive to the Oklahoma State Penitentiary, predictably called Big Mac, where Hobart Stubbs lived out his dwindling court-allotted days on death row. She was virtually his only visitor, Hobart having been abandoned by his family well before 1983.

She returned from these trips exhausted, almost unable to speak, at least not immediately. She'd go directly upstairs and run a bath. Adam once thought he heard her weeping behind the bathroom door. He waited in the kitchen. After she came out of the bath, however, she seemed oddly elated, glowing and serene, as if in the aftermath of a religious experience. She had evidently witnessed something in the long, narrow cell-lined hallways, under the fluorescents, under the meticulous scrutiny of armed guards, on the other side of the tempered glass, the immensity of which most people could only guess at.

She made a cup of green tea, a towel still wrapped around her head. Adam sat at the kitchen table with her.

"He's really the sweetest man imaginable, given that he's lived almost the hardest life imaginable," she said. "Adam, you have no idea. We've uncovered incidents of sexual abuse from the time he was *six*. An uncle. The uncle raped him possibly with the connivance of his father. Both parents on heroin. Living in an abandoned trailer. In and out of foster homes. There was evidence of intellectual disabilities going back to the time he was in grade school, and no one did anything for him. We have expert testimony that shows severe deficits in adaptive functioning, that he can't understand the case against him in a meaningful way. Yet he's unfailingly kind and thoughtful. He asked after you. He asked after Jason. He wanted to know how he was doing in school. This is a man on death row, a man the State of Oklahoma is determined to inject with lethal chemicals, possibly in a few weeks, and he wanted to know if my son is studying for his bar mitzvah!"

"What'd you tell him?"

"That of course he is."

Actually, the kid wasn't. Jason had totally slacked off with the haftorah. Adam was disproportionately annoyed that she had lied to the condemned man.

As a core belief, Adam knew that capital punishment was a barbaric measure. It was irreversible, and in many instances proof of innocence was uncovered after the fact. The punishment, like all criminal punishments in the United States, was applied at a rate against Black men like Hobart Stubbs considerably more often than it was against white men for the same offenses. It was applied against people with mental and physical disabilities. It brutalized society. Adam also knew that it was fundamental to the rule of law for everyone, the guilty as well as the innocent, to receive legal representation, and he was proud that Luann was nationally regarded as one of the best in her field. Few lawyers knew the case law as well as she did. No one was as strategically inventive.

Nevertheless, the specifics of the case stayed with Adam. The last thing that Vernon Hummel saw as his life slipped out of him was his daughter murdered.

And how severe could your deficits in adaptive functioning be if you knew about bar mitzvahs? In Oklahoma?

Luann said that his only hope now, with every circumstantial issue rejected, was for her to persuade the family of the victims to appeal for clemency.

"That's a lot to ask, don't you think?"

"It's a long shot," she conceded. "Of course, we'd have to demonstrate that he's a changed man. And he is. I'd have to arrange some kind of meeting with Astra. I'd have to lay it out for her. But she's born-again. We'd get her pastor involved. Mercy is a vital Christian value— and all we'd be asking for is a life sentence without parole. It's worth a try. This kind of intervention has been successful in the past."

"I meant that a meeting could be enormously painful for her."

"Adam," she said, her face darkening. "This is Hobart's last chance! If we don't do something, the

State of Oklahoma, acting with medieval vengeance, hypocritically and irresponsibly, will put the man to death. Believe me, I'm going to do everything I can to stop it."

Adam had already come to recognize that Luann had somehow begun to identify with Hobart Stubbs, even more than she had identified with previous defendants. Certainly no other person knew his personal history like she did. No one else had ever showed him such compassion. No one else, perhaps not even Hobart, feared the looming date of his execution to the same extent or imagined, coursing through his veins, first the sodium thiopental (to sedate him), then the pancuronium bromide (to paralyze his general muscle system), and finally the potassium chloride (to stop his heart).

The following morning, immediately after she woke up, or perhaps she had been up for hours, she called her client on death row, as she did every morning, from their bedside phone. This was a standing arrangement with the warden. Adam went to take a leak and put up the coffee. When he came back to their bedroom she had just hung up, visibly moved.

Adam thought it would come out like a joke when he said, "Hope you're not falling in love with him."

She didn't respond, not even to force a little air through her nose to indicate that she heard him. The expression on her face didn't change either, still showing the effects of the phone call. She was still inside her exchange with the convict. That was where she had decided she wanted to be. Then she rose to go to the bathroom too.

ADAM HAD LONG RECOGNIZED that, by any objective measure, Luann was an extremely time-challenged woman, often juggling more than one death penalty case at once. When she wasn't working on briefs, these cases almost fully occupied her mind. Her office was also rife with personal conflicts, and it could be argued (Adam argued this, to himself) that these disputes and struggles were intrinsically more compelling than the ones at the magazine, where for most of the week the writers were on their own and not necessarily on the premises. Some of *her* office's internal politics had life-and-death consequences. By now Adam was more intimate with the quirks of the lawyers, their assistants, and the secretarial staff than he was with those attached to some of his journalist colleagues.

Living with Luann, Adam had developed over the years what he thought was an advanced education in the criminal justice system, including a decent grounding in capital punishment law. He understood most of the ins and outs of what Luann was telling him and he was able to ask what he thought were pertinent questions. She answered them—at least the ones that were in fact pertinent—in the crisp, adamant, complete sentences of a law professor. She had once taught at Georgetown.

He had become increasingly aware that some of his recent work for the magazine lay beyond her range of concerns: about Ross Perot, about the Earned Income Tax Credit, about V-chips. A few months before, however, Adam had done a criminal justice piece that was at least adjacent to her interests. The article questioned the decade's "tough on crime" political consensus. Responding to the spread of crack cocaine and a surge in violent offenses, Clinton had signed the overwhelmingly bipartisan $30 billion 1994 Violent Crime Control and Law Enforcement Act, which included a "three strikes and you're out" provision for federal crimes. At least one premise of the bill was that the threat of sure and vigorous punishment would, by any conceivable logic, serve as a deterrent to crime. Few people would choose paths that inevitably led to prison. Surprisingly then, the prisons were now filling up, filling up so fast that there was hardly room for the new prisoners who had *not* been deterred. In the ten years since 1988, the US prison population had doubled to 1.2 million, disproportionately comprising African American men.

It was an important issue, so far hardly cresting into public awareness, and Max had liked the pitch, but Adam also knew that he was writing the story to appeal to Luann. They talked about it at length, like they used to, and she helped him clarify the problem. She put him in touch with some knowledgeable think tank people.

As he worked on the piece, Adam and Luann continued to discuss it. He reported every evening on whom he had spoken with that day. Sometimes she offered additional questions for follow-up. She made suggestions about how to structure the storytelling, convincing him not to open with an anecdotal lede. Even Jason started asking questions about mass incarceration. The boy thought he might do a project on it for his sixth-grade class. In these weeks, Adam realized, he was having more fun working on an article than he had in years, notwithstanding the hundreds of thousands of young Black men being stockpiled in the nation's prisons.

Adam's story grabbed the cover, with the headline "A Generation Behind Bars." He received a call from a *Washington Post* reporter and then a *Post* columnist, who would both cite the piece. (The *Times* picked up the subject but didn't mention the article, par for the course.) The White House ordered extra copies of the issue, though it couldn't have been satisfied with the article's main points. Clinton and other "Third Way" Democrats had won office with rhetoric about personal responsibility and support for mandatory sentencing. The campaign had especially appealed to urban Black voters who had been losing hope that Democrats cared about the violence and crime that afflicted their communities. It was this emphasis that had stanched the 1980s decline in Black turnout.

The day the magazine was published, however, a long-simmering personnel crisis in Luann's office came to a boil. She arrived home late. Jason had already gone to his computer. Luann was clearly wiped, her posture stooped, her hair spiraling down in front of her face. Adam met her in the hallway as she closed the front door.

"Edelstein's out! Sunil Khan's moving to mitigation! Everyone's carving out new turf. It's like Jets and Sharks."

"Jeez. I'll make you a drink."

She climbed out of her shoes and followed him into the kitchen, where he poured Scotch into two tumblers. She was still holding her briefcase. In a spirited, direct narrative, she gave him a detailed account of the sudden staffing shake-up, which was made up of many moving parts and had wide-ranging implications for the conduct of the office. Adam was familiar with most of the people involved. He knew on which sides they were arrayed. He could see the implications too. Luann's own place in the office was secure, and she might even have more of a free hand in the future, depending on where things fell out. It was too soon to tell. But today had been very dramatic. "I'm telling you, Adam, there was blood on the floor," she said, and meanwhile she had an appeal due Friday. She picked a lemony slice of chicken cutlet out of the pan.

"I can put it on a plate."

"Fuck it."

Waiting for her to come home, Adam had deliberated on whether he would show her the new issue tonight. He knew she would be tired. On the other hand, this was an article with which she had been closely involved. On a normal evening, it might have served as a little pick-me-up. But now she was obviously exhausted and distracted, almost unable to stand. But she saw the magazine on the kitchen counter.

"It's published," she observed. The affectless delivery of these two words confirmed how bone-tired she was.

"You can read it tomorrow."

She took another long sip from her glass, her hair still in her face. She hadn't even peed yet.

"You made the cover," she said. "Congratulations. I can read it now."

"It'll wait till tomorrow."

"Why not now?"

"The story's important," Adam said. "To me. And your suggestions were crucial. So I'm proud of the piece and," he added, knowing how needy he sounded, "I want you to give it the best read you can. Tomorrow'll be better."

She shrugged and went upstairs, unsteadily. He closed the downstairs lights and, in the dark, looked at the cover again. He wondered if she was aware that this was his fourteenth cover for the *Next Deal*.

The office turmoil continued for the rest of the week with new plotlines and sudden reversals of fortune. Arriving home in time for dinner the following night and the night after that, Luann was fatigued but also animated by the drama. She entertained Adam and Jason with stories tragic and funny, amusing them with the tight web of intrigue that had been enlaced within the underfunded local habeas section of a venerable civil rights organization.

Another day of office carnage followed. The new issue of the magazine remained on the kitchen counter where she had first seen it. He mentioned how the story had been picked up in other publications. He had heard from a staffer that the House Judiciary Committee might hold hearings. He may have been exaggerating the article's impact.

"That's great," she said vaguely, possibly confused for a moment about which article he was talking about. Then she remembered. She said, "Terrific. Can't wait to read it. Tonight!"

She finally opened the magazine that evening in bed, perhaps his least favorite place for her to read something he wrote, half reclined, but this was where in fact the *Next Deal* was meant to be read. Or it was meant to be read in an easy chair, or on the DC Metro or the Northeast Regional, or on the toilet. They *wrote* it for casual or semi-casual reading, for the lay reader, for the ordinary citizen with a good citizen's interest in politics and policy, and also for the well-rounded individual who cared about the arts and society. If anyone on the staff saw the magazine being read in the wild, they would make an announcement as soon as they arrived at work.

Luann may have been halfway to sleep, but she held a yellow highlighter with the magazine, the same highlighter she used to dissect legal briefs. This showed attentiveness. Then he was a little anxious about what the highlighter might find.

He looked away, pretending to read his book, but he imagined the words of the article as they passed beneath her eyes, how she understood them, what other personal associations they were making, and what articulated or unarticulated thoughts they might spark. He had previously performed this exercise, reading it with her eyes, while he was writing the piece.

He had enough time to get through a paragraph of his book, and get some sense from it, before she spoke.

"These figures. Are you not including undocumented migrants held in detention?"

"Well, they haven't been through the criminal justice system. It's a different category of custody."

She didn't comment, giving Adam plenty of time to wonder why she asked. He thought he had been clear about what the numbers represented. He hadn't wanted to throw apples and oranges into the same clink.

"And pretrial detention?"

"I included that. But read on. Everything will make sense."

The highlighter was still in her hand, but she hadn't uncapped it. He quickly glanced over. Unlike Max, she didn't frown, but the intensity of her reading was worrying enough. Those questions were worrying enough. How could she ask about pretrial detention?

"Wait, who told you that 'truth in sentencing' laws limit prison time?"

"It was in a report," he said vaguely. "The Brennan Center? You told me to look at it. Maybe it was Brookings."

She shook her head by about a millimeter and didn't speak again while she finished the article.

She put the highlighter on her night table and laid the article on her lap, staring across the bedroom. She was accustomed to highlighting everything: briefs, books, articles, and memos from Jason's school. She often fell asleep with the highlighter uncapped, inking blankets, sheets, and upholstery. You'd think someone would have invented a nonstaining highlighter by now. But she hadn't found anything worth highlighting in his piece, or perhaps she had simply found too much.

He said, "There were problems?"

She shook her head. "Just a couple of questions."

She didn't ask these questions. He didn't ask her to ask these questions. He didn't ask her if she liked the piece. She finally had to say something.

"The article is," she said, "good!"

He had heard the catch in her voice. The little pause, a tiny gap between words, was a chasm approximately the size of the Grand Canyon or the growing trade deficit with China, about which he had recently written.

"Thanks," he said, hiding his disappointment.

"I *enjoyed* it," she insisted, unable to hide her reserve. "It was *interesting*."

"But you didn't love it," he said, hating himself.

"I liked it," she insisted. "But you know, when you're so close to an issue . . ."

"This isn't exactly your issue. I got things wrong?"

"They're not important."

She handed the article back to him. He detected a weary effort, as if the magazine was the weight of the Sunday *Times*.

"You know," she said, "charging inmates fees for their incarceration isn't limited to for-profit prisons."

"But that's part of their business model."

"Not exclusively."

He said, "I thought we went over it. 'Pay to stay.' I got that wrong?"

"I guess you didn't understand what I said. My fault, probably. Lawyers are just too immersed in the law. It makes it hard to express yourself to an ordinary citizen."

Adam thought of himself as something more than an ordinary citizen. He wondered if somebody would write in to complain. Max would be irritated.

"I don't think it rises to the level of a correction," he said firmly, though he wasn't sure. It was best to wait for a complaint. The magazine's response would depend on the letter and especially on the significance of the person who wrote it, either political or academic. Adam would have to present Max with an argument against the complaint. Max wouldn't want to acknowledge a mistake or run the letter, yet at the same time he would go to great lengths to show that he didn't think the magazine was above criticism. So he would run the letter, sulking. "I'm sorry you didn't care for the piece," Adam told Luann. "I was pretty satisfied."

"The article's good," she repeated. "It's me. When you're involved with criminal justice, you know it inside and out. First there's theory, then there's history, and then there's the letter of the law itself—all of it working together like an intricate, exquisitely tuned mechanism, even when it's not working humanely or justly. We *hope* we can turn the machine toward justice. And then a journalist comes along and takes it apart to what they think are the essentials. But the machine can't work on essentials. So it's shocking when you see what they leave out. How much nuance is lost. I'm sure the same thing happens when journalists summarize issues in other fields, like politics, medicine, or women's tennis. That's the problem, not your piece, which really, Adam, is very good and, most importantly, it advances the conversation."

Adam nodded, not fully mollified.

She added, "The key thing is that the story reported about more than the strain on the prison system. You have that section about the impact on children and families. Mass incarceration is changing society in ways we're just starting to appreciate. But journalism will always skate on the surface of an issue. That doesn't make journalism not worthwhile, Adam. I know how vital, how integral, it is to democracy."

"Right," Adam said emphatically. "It is."

Was that the turning point for them? He didn't know, but her comments stuck with him. He knew she was essentially correct about the limitations of journalism (though no one complained about the article and they never ran a correction). He got things wrong all the time. He misquoted people, very often because he couldn't read his own goddamn notes. Or he didn't always understand what the people he interviewed meant to say, or he didn't ask the right questions, or he didn't really understand the issue. The truth of the story he was telling often seemed to elude him, shimmering inches away, just beyond his grasp. The finished article would be an approximation of something. And then it fell into the unending churn of news and opinion, on the way to irrelevance. Only rarely could he watch a piece of his reporting touch anything in the real world. And he *still* couldn't read his goddamn notes.

Shortly after he did the prison piece, Luann took on the Hobart Stubbs case. In the next several months, as she became ever more involved with the condemned man, she may have begun to withdraw from family life, though the withdrawal was so slight Adam may have been imagining it, the fantasy a product of his own self-involvements.

He watched her when Jason asked for help with his homework. Did Adam see reluctance or an impatience with him? Did Jason? Jason now seemed to be approaching his father more often for help with his non-Spanish homework. Adam thought he was also going to Luann less frequently for Spanish, a language in which she was fluent, but that might have been because the boy had finally come to understand the differences between the two states-of-being verbs, *ser* and *estar.*

In the following months nothing was really settled at Luann's office as the conflicts there multiplied and engendered new iterations. Although these squabbles were wearying, her position was untouched, and she was allowed to do her work. She was now drilling down deeper into the Stubbs case. She was receiving the first intimations of prosecutorial error. She had also dug up some records pertaining to Hobart's youth that were incomplete and unclear, as if he were a minor figure from the early Middle Ages, his name sometimes misspelled, his birthdate reported variously, in the microfilmed archives of the county social welfare agencies, such as they were. She had begun visiting him on death row. The office imbroglios were trivial games, given the magnitude of her contest against the State of Oklahoma.

AT THE END of the following century's second decade, the *Next Deal* was trending, unhappily. Adam was still staring at a feed laser-targeted to his political affinities, personal proclivities, consumer behavior, conceits, fatuities,

specific tastes in the occasional cheesecake bot, and ruin-
ous deficits of character.

The morning after Valerie's run-in with Max, Adam
had mentioned it to his wife, reporting everything Valerie
had told him. They were at breakfast. Luann laughed,
still turning the pages of the newspaper.

"What a jerk!"

Adam had apparently turned the story into an amusing anecdote, something for which he had a natural
inclination. He hadn't meant to.

To make up for it, he emphasized, "She was very hurt
and angry."

"I don't blame her."

"What should she do?"

She looked up from the newspaper briefly.

"What can she do? She wants to keep writing for
the magazine, right? She has to get over it. This happens to women all the time. I've put up with all kinds
of crap."

Adam recalled Luann's experience as a woman in
the several law offices through which she had passed,
and then back to law school. She had frequently been
undervalued and condescended to. She had told him
about certain unpleasant encounters with male colleagues and expressed various degrees of annoyance
and distress. Some of these encounters, according to
the changing mores of the late 1990s, could have now
been termed harassment, but they weren't exactly of the

kind Valerie had suffered the day before. Luann had received no romantic propositions from her supervisors, as far as he knew. He wondered if there were incidents he didn't know about. There had been a time when he and Luann told each other everything. That moment may have passed. The stories she now brought back from the office were less personal, usually involving the specifics of her work. Adam had reported the full story of Valerie and Max, but he had left out the part about the embrace at the Metro station.

"Men are idiots," he said.

"Yeah," Luann replied. "I know."

A new warrant of execution was served, the McAlester warden arriving at Hobart's cell and reading it to the prisoner himself, as required by legal protocol. Luann said that she would have to go to Oklahoma and remain on hand while her office pursued a series of appeals. The local ACLU lawyers needed her presence. Hobart needed her there too.

Adam wondered about her delivery of this announcement. As Hobart Stubbs's time ran out, Luann hadn't mentioned that anything was imminent. If the warrant had been issued earlier today, she could have called Adam from the office. She could have told him when she arrived home. When he asked her about her day, she had been a little evasive, now that he thought about it. And now she chose to reveal her assignment at dinner, to her husband and son at the same time. Adam realized that he and Luann had suddenly embarked on a journey into new marital territory.

"I'll call every night," she said, looking directly at Jason. "You boys are going to do fine without me."

"Right," Adam assured him, as if he had already known. "It'll be fun. I'll be home, I'll help you with your homework if you need it. Maybe we'll do a hiking trip, out to Shenandoah? Go up to Camden Yards and catch the O's? But if you don't learn your fucking haftorah, I'm going to murder you in your sleep."

Luann continued to stare at the boy. Adam thought he may have seen tears collecting in her eyes. She was deliberately not looking at Adam. It was as if she had erected a barrier at the left side of her face, so that she couldn't see him. She was also looking past their son, beyond the Beltway, beyond the low mountains and vast plains that came next, all the way to another person sitting alone in a concrete-walled, windowless room the size of a parking space.

Jason said, "Knife or pillow?"

Getting ready for bed later, Adam mentioned his surprise to Luann. She responded by emphasizing the degree of injustice that was being perpetrated and explaining again how important the case was. She said it might eventually go to the Supreme Court. She insisted that Hobart required her presence, that he was utterly alone, and that he understood, finally, the absolute terror of his situation. Her words were compassionate but her manner was cold, edging into anger, as if Adam were challenging her or, God forbid, defending the death penalty. He pretended not to notice.

But he doubted the case presented enough constitutional issues to get anywhere near First Street. He took her assertion as further evidence that she was losing perspective on the case, and not only on the case. The preoccupation that had turned into an obsession was also a displacement.

VALERIE'S GLOBAL WARMING STORY ran in the next issue. She took on another assignment, but she stayed away from the office. As she told Adam, she no longer wanted to be alone with Max. She hadn't been alone with him since the day he made the pass, though she had to show up in the magazine's conference room for last week's all-hands meeting about coverage of the 2000 election.

"I couldn't look him in the eyes. It's like everything I thought about him, everything he was for me, has been erased. I began subscribing to the magazine in high school! I've read every editorial he's written since then. And once I came to Washington I couldn't believe I was writing for him. I couldn't stop telling Max-stories to my friends, about his piercing insights, about his intricate phrasings, about his political nonconformism, about the way he makes a beeline for the doughnuts when we have them. What I was *really* doing was boasting that I knew him. But now he gives me the creeps. I can't look him in the eyes," she repeated, "and that's what he was trying to make me do. All of us were in the room, talking about Bill Bradley and the caucuses, blah-blah-blah, but he kept on turning to me, and I'm not even on staff. I had to turn away, as if I were the guilty one. Now I'll never get on staff."

She and Adam talked nearly every night on the phone and continued to meet for lunch, at least once a week and then at least twice. Even as the episode with Max receded, she seemed off balance, unsure about how to proceed with her career. She asked about possible stories, how to frame them, and who she should call. Adam shot down one or two ideas but mostly encouraged her. She welcomed his encouragement. He told her how many words the pieces would need. She also asked for personal advice in the aftermath of her breakup with Josef. She needed some encouragement there too. Adam's advice about that was probably boilerplate. She said she was going to take some time off from dating. She needed to rethink what she wanted. He nodded in a way that he hoped was supportive, and not too sage-like. When it came to her romantic life she sounded somewhere close to bereft.

He joked about how he and Jason were struggling not to turn into complete slobs while Luann was in Oklahoma. He insisted they were eating right and picking up after themselves. Not that Luann ever picked up after them, he asserted. The kid was doing his homework, getting a little fresh air, and losing his immortal soul to the internet. The only big change was that they were leaving the toilet seat up.

"You talk to her?"

"She has tons of work," he said. "Writing briefs and petitions. Making calls. They're pulling every lever that's there, some levers that are not, and some levers that are only figments of their imagination. She spends nearly every visiting hour with him on death row. But she knows we'll call her if there's a reason."

Adam saw her antennae go up. She was a sharp young woman. She was also a good reporter, former managing editor of the *Yale Daily News* (as he would not need to be reminded twenty years later), and she would listen for weaknesses in one's statements as a matter of course, which was annoying as hell.

"How often *does* she speak with you?"

"As needed," he confessed. "Last week we had to talk about getting our gutters cleaned," he added lamely. "Honestly, Valerie, this case has dominated her life like nothing she's ever done before. Everything else has been pushed into the background, into the shadows." He paused, unsure that he wanted to go on. She waited, a reporter's trick. He said, "We may have been drifting apart before then."

He hated to be admitting this, or to be admitting any kind of personal trouble at all. He was reminded now that Valerie was twelve years younger than he was and in a different part of her life. In her company he had sought to play the older, settled, more experienced friend. He liked to think he impressed her with the life he had built with Luann and Jason, and that it offered a vision of her own productive adult future.

She was gazing at him now, intently but softly. She reached across the table and squeezed him by the hand. Her hand was warm and he squeezed back, then was jolted by the unexpected charge that ran through him, a blast of light and heat that extended from his core to the extremities, blinding him for a moment. Something opened up in him, something, a door, that he hadn't known was closed. The feeling was almost painful.

Meanwhile the planet's atmosphere was warming. So were the oceans, apparently, and, according to Valerie, the waters' higher temperatures were doing more than melting icebergs. They were rerouting currents, heightening salinization in certain ocean regions and at certain depths, and damaging sensitive undersea habitats. Scientists were warning about massive fish and other marine die-offs. Valerie had begun working on the story, collecting oceanographic charts and maps, too many to be spread out on a table in a coffee shop. She needed to talk it over. One afternoon while Adam was waiting for edits on a story of his own, she asked him to come to the apartment she shared with a young woman who covered arts for the alt weekly *City Paper.*

It was located in the Kalorama neighborhood, in a midcentury fieldstone apartment building near some foreign embassies. The building was handsome, but the apartment itself was closer to a grad student's space, its hallways furnished with framed posters for old newspaper movies like *His Girl Friday* and *Deadline-U.S.A.* The place had a small functional kitchen with painted wood cabinets, a Frigidaire that looked like a 1950s Buick, and a counter with two bar stools. After taking some direct hits here and there, the floor tile was finely spidered. He observed the absence of a dishwasher.

She asked if he wanted tea, and when he said no, she whisked him into her bedroom.

This was a much larger space, with high ceilings and a big sunlit window overlooking the street. A colorful Turkish kilim covered the parquet and opposite the window hung a framed print of something dark and Middle Eastern. CDs were lined on the floor beneath the window. Her desktop computer rested on a long beige Ikea desk, the same desk he had laboriously assembled for Jason. A few large black-and-white scientific maps were spread out on the white cotton bedspread, the bed in the center of the room, against the far wall. She had straightened up in advance of his arrival, and no underclothes were strewn about, but this was certainly a bedroom inhabited by a woman. On her dresser, which was also from Ikea, there were several personal photographs in frames and on the frames she had draped some necklaces.

"Welcome to my boudoir."

He didn't have a comeback for that—he was too intensely aware that he was in her boudoir. Although the queen-size bed was obscured by maps, the idea of the bed dominated the room. It was a low bed, easy to fall into, with maroon throw pillows accentuating the colors in the kilim. Sunlight splayed across the maps. A night table on the side was neatly stacked with a variety of current affairs magazines, not only the *Next Deal*. Adam's most recent cover story was on top, which would have given him some satisfaction if he were not distracted by the bed.

She was wearing one of her white button-down shirts. He saw that study of the maps would demand some physical contortions from them both. The two journalists would have to rest on the bed together, close, as they examined depth and temperature contour lines. He'd lean here, she'd lean there, almost like a game of Twister. They'd be aware of each other's temperatures and contours. Books lay open on her desk. He and Valerie would rise to the desk to look at them, too, over each other's shoulders. He resolved to stay on the right side of her body.

The hours would pass slowly, experienced as parallel time units by the two brains at work in his single skull. One was trying to process the organization of the story she was planning to write, to figure out what further reporting she would have to do. This probably meant *limiting* the story, possibly to the threat posed to commercial fisheries—not exactly a hot topic, but he was still unsure that the warming of the oceans was more than a fringe issue. He himself preferred swimming in warm water. The other brain seemed to be located in an entirely different part of his head. This brain was overwhelmed by sensation, not only of their body heat, but also of her scent, even if she didn't wear perfume. Maybe it was the lip gloss. He would soon ascertain that she was wearing a short black bra today, either as a provocation or as protection against his spying eyes, he didn't know.

They didn't kiss that afternoon nor the next nor the one after that, though every time he returned to the office, increasingly late in the day, he asked himself why not, with increasing urgency. Actually, there were several good solid reasons why not, as many good reasons as there were for the Comprehensive Nuclear-Test-Ban Treaty, for example. He tried not to list them. Every reason seemed to argue against his personhood. He had a vague sense of what it must feel like to have one's personal interests commit you to the wrong side of an issue.

He gave some thought now to *Valerie's* personal interest. She would have been aware of their growing closeness, physical and otherwise. She, too, might have wondered if there would be a kiss. Adam hadn't seen any indication that this was what she wanted; her warmth and friendliness wasn't necessarily flirtatious, though he wasn't entirely sure he knew that it wasn't. He guessed that she believed *he* wasn't showing romantic

interest either. He, too, hadn't been necessarily flirtatious. Maintaining their non-romantic friendship was
obviously important to him. Oh yeah, and he was married. But she was just as capable of self-delusion as anyone else, simply because she liked having him there.

The other possibility was that she was waiting for
Adam, waiting for him to make an unambiguous move.
This was what was generally expected. In the movies
at least, it usually involved the man's uninvited attempt
at a kiss.

He would come to wish that he had kissed her then.
Things would have been less complicated.

After they initially sketched out the story, Valerie didn't
really need him to come over, but he did anyway. They
continued to have an appetite for each other's company;
it might have even been called a hunger. He became
familiar with the selection of her teas, the resistance
exerted by her toilet flusher lever, and the way her face
lit when he arrived. It lit unambiguously. One afternoon
they contrived to read some printed reports while sitting
on the bed back-to-back. It wasn't exactly a comfortable
position, but the weight and warmth of her body was
continually transmitted to his, as was every flinch and
adjustment in her posture. He discovered that the print
on the wall was from a painting of an odalisque in artful
dishabille, by Matisse. The pictures on the dresser featured her parents and grandparents.

After she sent in a draft, Max told Adam he was impressed by the way the story was turning out. He had just a few notes.

"You're helping her with this?"

Adam shrugged. "A little."

Max gazed at him owlishly. Adam felt fully penetrated by his regard. "Are you like . . . *mentoring* her?"

"C'mon, Max," Adam said in dismissal. "She's a full-fledged reporter. You should put her on staff already. I'm just giving the piece another set of eyes."

The editor didn't shift his study of him. These days the word *mentor* had taken on a suspect tone, though it wasn't as charged as the word *intern*.

Max observed, "She's very attractive."

"Sure," Adam said quickly, overdoing his show of indifference. Max would see that. But Adam also wanted to head off any man-to-man discussion of Valerie's corporeal virtues. Or her essential physicality. He wouldn't have thought Max was as crude as that, but after the editor's pass at the young woman, he wasn't sure. Adam would have thought himself more likely to be as crude as that. He added, "Very cute. She has a boyfriend. Luann and I went out with them."

Max absorbed this information but wasn't satisfied. "How *is* Luann?"

Adam wondered if this question was meant to remind him that he was married; it was amazing how easy that was to forget. If so, Max might be simply warning him from complicating his life. Or he might be trying to head off a potential romantic rival—if Max really thought of himself as a credible suitor. Did *Adam* think of himself as a credible suitor? Not really, he reminded himself.

"She's good," he said. "Deeply involved in a big death penalty case. But they're running out of options." Then Adam added, recklessly, "She's been sent to Oklahoma."

This information didn't alter Max's expression, but he said, "Where the wind comes sweepin' down the plain."

Adam said, "No, the other one."

Max looked again at the printout. He turned a couple of pages.

"Well, whatever you did on the story, I'm glad you got involved. You two are very friendly, huh?"

Max was suspicious again, now that he knew Luann was away. It was also possible that Max was fishing, trying to determine whether Valerie told him about the pass. No, Adam thought, Max was unlikely to expect that. Max was from a marginally older generation whose men and women, if they were only friends, didn't share such confidences. And Max may not have been aware that what he thought was a romantic gesture had crossed any lines worth talking about.

"I like her a lot," Adam said openly, happily, with some confidence that *his* generation had a healthier approach to male-female friendships. "She's a friend."

Years later, well before the *Politico* story, Adam would realize that this was the moment he should have brought up the pass. He could have spoken of it vaguely, just to let Max know Valerie was hurt and that he knew about the incident. It would have been a warning. But Max would have been furious that Adam was interfering with his personal life. In the course of their long professional association, the two men would go on to tell each other to go fuck themselves a total of seven times, but none of that had happened yet.

Now the editor said, "She should talk to Larissa about art. It's going to be a problem."

"We have some oceanographic charts. They're kind of beautiful in their own way. Maybe she can crop a couple or do something stylized."

The *we* was inadvertent. Max had noticed it.

BILL CLINTON'S IMPEACHMENT trial had ended just a few months earlier with his acquittal on charges that he had obstructed justice and lied to a grand jury about his affair with a White House intern, Monica Lewinsky. Lewinsky had performed fellatio on the president several times in a study outside the Oval Office. The two also engaged in phone sex. As the affair cooled, she was moved to a job at the Pentagon, where she became friends with a coworker, Linda Tripp, who secretly recorded the young woman's account of the liaison. Tripp passed more than twenty hours of tapes to independent counsel Kenneth Starr, who was originally appointed to investigate an unrelated real estate deal with which the Clintons were involved in the 1970s. The tapes were also made available to the lawyers for a former Arkansas state employee, Paula Jones, who claimed that in 1991 the then governor Clinton had exposed himself to her in a Little Rock hotel room. In a deposition for the sexual harassment suit, Jones's lawyers asked the president about the affair with Lewinsky. He denied that they had sexual relations. Once this statement leaked, Clinton adamantly repeated the denial to his wife, his cabinet, and the public. He maintained his denial even when Lewinsky produced a semen-stained navy-blue dress. DNA tests eventually proved that the semen had once belonged to the president.

Almost nothing about the affair had amused Adam's colleagues more than the assertion by the president of the United States, in his deposition, that what went on between him and Lewinsky did not qualify as sexual relations.

Charlotte Skinner read from the August 16, 1998, *Times* article: "Sexual relations were defined as 'contact with the genitalia, anus, groin, breast, inner thigh or buttocks of any person with an intent to arouse or gratify the sexual desire of any person.' By a literal reading, that definition would not embrace the passive partner in oral sex, who could say truthfully that he had not had sexual relations."

The women were laughing with tears in their eyes. How was a blow job *not* sexual relations? Was there some question about what qualified as a blow job? Did it mean taking the whole shaft? What if you just licked the tip? If the guy didn't come, was it still a blow job? How good did a blow job have to be to qualify as sex? Larissa Karapetyan said sourly that she could think of several instances of oral sex, not blow jobs, that really hadn't qualified as sex. There was enough merriment in the office to think that someone had won the lottery.

His ears burning, Adam kept out of it. He had several minds about the case, reflecting shifting progressive opinion. Obviously, Clinton and Lewinsky were consenting adults and what they did in their private lives should have remained private. And, also obviously, Clinton was the victim of an overzealous independent prosecutor. But still, he should have known better. Adam wished commentary about the president's dick wasn't in the papers.

His twelve-year-old son was now reading the *Times* at breakfast, this unfolding story the first time he had taken an interest in political affairs. He read from page one to the jump, all the sidebars, and all the pieces on the op-ed page. William Safire was having the time of his life. Adam was left with the sports pages. Luann was upstairs, getting dressed for the office.

Jason closed the paper.

He said, "What's the big deal?"

"Clinton had a relationship with a woman who was not his wife. That was wrong," Adam said delicately. "It had nothing to do with his conduct as president, but the Republicans are going to use it against him. They want to drive him from office and cripple the Democrats on values."

The boy grinned.

"This is about a blow job? So what, she gave him a blow job."

Adam had hoped not to get down to specifics.

"More than one. But yeah, you're right—it's nobody's business. The problem is that he lied about it under oath."

"Wouldn't you?"

Adam looked away, embarrassed about being placed in this scenario, embarrassed that his son was speculating about his father getting a blow job. From a woman who was not his mother. Not that he would want Jason speculating about his father getting a blow job from his mother. *Goddamn you, Bill Clinton.*

"Look," Adam said. "It's perjury, regardless of his motives. The Republicans have him right where they want him."

"But he didn't lie," Jason declared. "A blow job isn't really sexual relations."

Adam scowled at the boy. He was really a boy, still underweight, his teenage growth surge still somewhere in the indefinite future. It was possible that he would never stand taller than his father.

"Most adults think it is. The legal definition may have a loophole. Clinton knew that when he testified."

"People at school get blow jobs all the time," Jason exclaimed. "They don't think twice about it!"

"Maybe they should."

"I mean, it's part of a normal, healthy sex life."

Adam didn't really believe it was part of a middle schooler's normal, healthy sex life, not at Georgetown Day. He didn't know what went on in the public schools.

Jason continued, delighted with his father's discomfort. "People do it on first dates. It's kind of a thing at bar mitzvahs, too, for the kid getting bar mitzvahed. It's like a rite of passage. 'Today you are a man.' Josh Rabinowitz got one at his."

"Yeah, right."

This conversation rattled Adam the rest of the morning. This wasn't the first time he had heard of the relaxing attitudes about fellatio among young people, especially teenage girls. The *Times* had run a story. The theme was amplified with great excitement in general interest magazines like *New York* and *Vanity Fair*. What had once been a profoundly intimate sexual act had now been relocated to somewhere between second and third base. Adam didn't know anything about the psychological and social science, but he was sure that middle schoolers were too young to be engaged in such intimacies. Certainly, especially among twelve-, thirteen-, and fourteen-year-olds, there were issues involving intimidation and coercion. These same issues motivated concerns about pedophilia. Still, if you were assigned the study, song, and memorization of Hosea 14—"*Shuvah yis'rael ad y'hwah eloheykha Kiy khashal'Ta Baawonekha!* O Israel, return unto the

Lord thy God; for thou hast fallen by thine inequity"—
it was a hell of an incentive.

THE SCANDAL had provided an opportunity for the
Next Deal to rejuvenate its nonconformist notoriety.
After the Lewinsky story broke, Max called a meeting
of the senior writers: Adam, Charlotte Skinner, Quentin
Harper, and Samuel Wishniak. He didn't announce the
subject of the meeting. They filed into his private office,
taking seats on the two upholstered chairs and the low
couch. The long window opposite Max's desk looked
out on the Capitol dome, almost incandescent under the
sun, a sight that always raised Adam's spirits, no matter
who held the majority beneath it.

The editor let them get settled. Adam occupied the
couch with Skinner, who wore a snug, mid-calf skirt,
the only woman in the office who regularly wore skirts.
She had terrific long legs that had once sprinted her
across a mine-encrusted Chechen field under Russian
fire and which she now extended as if working on a tan.
Charlotte and Adam routinely took the couch at the
editorial meetings, just as Quentin and Samuel always
took the chairs. The seating arrangement may have
indicated something about the magazine's hierarchy,
even if the writers were grouped alphabetically in the
staff box.

Max studied them for a few moments, a thoughtful
smile playing around his lips.

Finally he said, "OK, my friends, what do we think about Bill Clinton these days?"

This was a gigantic question, of course, as Max intended it to be. In Washington, if not across America, you were thinking about the president all the time, whoever the president was. Even before he was president, as he was campaigning for the office, you came to know the man's biography as intimately as a friend's or lover's, and how his character expressed itself as he faced issues personal and political. During his term in office, his character would be further tested by crisis. Books would be written about what was then revealed. The president would come to mean something, or rather he would take on a host of meanings, some of them defining the age. The president, and what you thought of him, defined who *you* were in the years of his administration.

Charlotte said, "Well, since I learned it was bent . . ."

This was an old, puerile joke, though at the moment not irrelevant, dating from the Paula Jones case. Jones claimed that among the "distinguishing characteristics" of the erect penis offered to her by Governor Clinton was its curvature, a painful symptom caused by a condition named Peyronie's disease. No medical evidence had been produced suggesting that the president was in fact so afflicted.

There were some titters, even from Samuel, who was a serious young law school graduate. Even when Skinner wasn't especially funny you laughed so that you wouldn't seem sanctimonious and, also, so that you wouldn't embarrass her. She was universally admired by the Washington press corps, for her sources and for the tenacity of her reporting. She had broken several of the Newt Gingrich stories, including his misuse of tax-exempt donations for political purposes. Skinner did the Mae West act to hide her flint, which is what Mae West had done, both women performing the concealment with limited success.

Max said, "I'm glad we got that out of the way."

"Max, Clinton's a dope, and so is she, but she's not a child," Skinner said. "They had an affair. That's between them, and between Bill and Hillary—really, what do we know about the state of the Clinton marriage? Or how they define what's permissible in their individual sex lives? This whole thing is about sexual repression and it plays into the hands of those who would infantilize women, mostly men, men who would prohibit them from making their own sexual choices. The Puritans, the ayatollahs, the Moral Majority. Remember, *she* seduced *him*. I talk to Europeans and they think we're behaving like children ashamed of our body parts and our natural desires."

Quentin added, "It's an unfortunate situation, but our natural prurient interest has distracted us from what's really at stake. Hillary is correct, it *is* a 'vast, right-wing conspiracy,' to destroy this presidency and the Democratic Party. Billionaires funded the original Clinton investigations. Lewinsky was illegally taped. Starr improperly

questioned her about a consensual relationship that had
nothing to do with the Jones case, let alone Whitewater.
He set a perjury trap. Then the grand jury testimony was
leaked. It's all being done to get Clinton."

Adam liked Quentin, even though he was just slum-
ming at the magazine. He'd be leaving soon, possibly
to return to Harvard or to join one of the main papers'
editorial boards. Adam thought he and Skinner had correctly articulated Adam's own feelings.

"You've convinced me," Max said. "Clinton has to go."

"Max!" Quentin protested.

Other murmurs of dissent were voiced around the
room.

"It's a vast, right-wing conspiracy," Max agreed ami-
ably. "And it was successful, at least in the short run. So
they beat Clinton. He should resign. It's one of the foun-
dational principles of representational democracy: if you
get caught with your pants down, you're out. Charles
Stewart Parnell. John Profumo. Japanese prime minister Sōsuke Uno. It's not a values issue. It's simply that
the party is more important than its individual members, whatever their degree of curvature. The Clinton
agenda—strengthening Social Security and Medicare,
expanding child health care, expanding access to higher
education, gun safety—is more important than Clinton.
Give Al Gore a year of incumbency. The economy's
strong, 4.6 percent unemployment, the first budget sur-
plus since 1969. He'll be the heavy favorite for 2000."

"That would be tragically unfair," Samuel complained. "The Republicans are monumental hypocrites. Newt Gingrich is on his second wife, but continues to date his staffers. He left his first wife for a younger woman while she was in the hospital for cancer surgery. Dan Burton, Bob Barr, all involved with other women. The Republicans have gone beyond a double standard. Now they're applying the law of the jungle. It's pure power unattached to principle."

Max shrugged. For Max, the unfairness of life was something great, something majestic, something literary: a reminder of human insignificance. The unfairness of politics was a trivial instance of human insignificance. The unfairness of some politician losing his job after getting sucked off by an intern was a triviality of spectacular minuteness. But you couldn't give up on politics, Max believed. Compassionate, imaginative, optimistic politics occasionally managed to better the human condition. He would make this the final point of his lead editorial.

Now Adam saw that Max was right. The call for Clinton's resignation would hit the news cycle like a bomb. All the papers would carry it. Max would repeat these points on the cable news programs in his usual sphinxlike mode, speaking softly in fully formed sentences, with tremendous breath control, smiling condescendingly at the host's objections. The White House would push back, of course, but they might begin to hear whispers from congressional and party leaders. It may have also occurred to Adam that Al Gore's rise to the presidency would make the hiring of a staff environmental reporter all the more timely.

BUT CLINTON HADN'T taken Max's advice, just as he hadn't taken his earlier advice about gays in the military and Travelgate, and, a year later, after a brutal, humiliating impeachment trial, he was still in office and Valerie was still working freelance.

As if they were newlyweds, she and Adam hardly left the bedroom. She needed help with Max's further questions about the ocean-warming story. Adam brought his laptop to her apartment to work on his own piece. It had been difficult to focus at the office, in her absence. Now they faced each other at opposite ends of her surprisingly stable desk, laptop plugs snugly side by side in the outlet beneath the desk. When they went to the kitchen for tea, they came back with it.

Adam was of course just as aware of Valerie's presence as he had been at the office. More aware. He looked up over his screen, surreptitiously or not, and there she was, her eyes fixed on her own screen. Like Luann, but totally unlike Adam, she was almost undistractible. Adam was as free to study her as if she were in a film. He could watch her think or watch her expression change as she found the phrase she was looking for. Or watch her being stumped. Sometimes she looked up and didn't see him at all, blind to her surroundings. Other times she did see him. She smiled, absently. He detected warmth around her eyes. He listened to her breathe faintly through her mouth. In these moments, he had no idea what he was working on.

She rose from her chair and moved around the room to pick up a book, gaze again at a map laid out on the bed, open or close a window, travel to the bathroom or to the kitchen, activating each limb and every part of her torso. After he had arrived that day he watched her crawl under the desk to grab the cord from his laptop and insert the plug. The top of her underwear rode up over her jeans. They were good sturdy pastel-pink cotton briefs, but they affected him no less than would have the skimpiest thong.

When he did manage to knuckle down and finish a draft, he emailed it across the desk. She read it, grimacing like Max did. He wondered if she had learned this from Max. Adam probably grimaced like that too. Unlike Max, she rarely questioned the premise of a piece, but she was good with missing transition sentences and loosely constructed phrases. She was always on the lookout for an unclear or unvoiced thought, something hidden within the text. She would mutter, almost to herself, "What are you trying to tell me?"

Even after Yale, Valerie had retained the down-to-earthness he associated with the city of Philadelphia. Her father was the manager of a furniture showroom; her mother did something secretarial at Blue Cross—so they weren't text-book working class, but they were at home in the South Philly of aluminum-sided row houses, hoagie shops, string bands, Eagles devotion, and multigenerational neighbor-hood feuds over on-street parking spaces. They were party-line Democrats. Subscribing to the *Next Deal*, even if they found the articles awfully theoretical, her parents read every word she published. The glossy paper made them think she was being paid extravagantly. She wasn't, but she loved writing for the magazine. She had fallen into the environmental beat because it seemed like a good continu-ing story. She had no particular affinity for nature. She had never been to the Billy Goat Trail or Theodore Roosevelt Island. She had kept her South Philly accent.

Adam knew something was strange about the chaste intimacy they had adopted, even if close, easygoing friendships between men and women were a significant feature of late twentieth-century cosmopolitan mores. Yet sexual promiscuity, as a temptation and a *good thing*, was also elemental to these mores, at least as he understood them from popular culture and other social signals. He and Valerie both maintained conventional, fairly permissive liberal attitudes about sex, he assumed. He saw the authors represented in her tall non-Ikea wal-nut bookcase: D. H. Lawrence, Edna O'Brien, Jeanette Winterson, Erica Jong, Tama Janowitz, Alice Walker, Nicholson Baker, the Marquis de Sade. None of them had done much with chaste intimacy.

Her roommate came home from work early one afternoon and the two journalists emerged from the bedroom so that Valerie could introduce him to her. Adam thought he behaved in an ordinarily friendly way, offering his hand. For a moment the young woman seemed leery about taking it. She blushed and giggled, and Valerie was flustered, too, as if what had been going on in the bedroom, as if what they were still straightening their clothes from, was a total fuckfest. That was what anyone, meeting him in that situation, would have expected. Her roommate might have been wondering where his hand had just been.

DAMN. NOW THERE WAS a new hashtag: *#Unsubscribe NDeal*. Readers were canceling their subscriptions, supposedly. The likes had reached 110K, more subscribers than the magazine had.

Adam made another cup of coffee, waiting for an email or a text. Both the *Times* and the *Post* were probably working on stories. He was slightly miffed that they hadn't contacted him yet. He could guess who would be doing the stories. They were pretty experienced reporters and they hadn't figured out, like the youngster Singleton, that he was on staff at the magazine in 1999. Bad legwork.

Or possibly the story wasn't as big as Twitter made it out to be. Twitter didn't represent the entire media environment, of course. Neither did the *Times* nor the *Post*. You had to listen to what was being said on the cable news shows. Even then, you didn't know what was important to anyone beyond the Beltway. Or whether there was anyone beyond the Beltway. The question of what was really news, what really defined news, hovered in the mists above the Potomac. Anyway, CNN hadn't picked up the story. They probably wouldn't without a clip of Valerie or at least a headshot.

He began to think it was safe to plan the day ahead. He had to make some further calls for the new piece. He also had to finish the delicate composition of his covertly wheedling note to Nuri Gelman, the network exec. The flow of tweets seemed to have let up. At least *#Lieberlover* was flat. It was a lame hashtag anyway.

That was the operative thought for about four foolish minutes. Singleton would be proven right of course: the story had legs. In about 240 seconds, refreshing his feed, Adam would discover that the story was the fucking Rockettes.

Valerie was on the record now in her own words, which were being furiously tweeted. She had posted a piece on the Cut, the women-oriented site published by *New York* magazine. When he clicked on the link, he felt some corresponding thud in his lower intestines. Valerie had taken control of the narrative.

"Same Old Deal at the Same Old *Next Deal*."

Adam began reading. He saw that Valerie was confirming the *Politico* story and intended to elaborate on it, publishing the article as a personal essay. Fair game. The top was gracefully but urgently written, going beyond her experiences at the magazine to encompass the entire culture of Washington journalism as she found it when she arrived in the late 1990s. She had been unprepared for the male-dominated, sexually aggressive environment.

It was a long piece. He Ctrl-F'd his name.

Nothing.

He did it again, just to make sure.

But he still had to read on, starting with her introductory argument that the sexism built into American journalism extended well beyond sexual harassment. Sexism was why the media had always failed to cover women's issues properly. Adam thought this was a little unfair, considering the many women-oriented stories that had been broken by men, including himself (pay disparities among congressional staffers; the anti-choice implications obscured within a new Mississippi hospital staffing law). But he also thought the charge was fair too. Society was always coming late to things that mattered to more than half the population. He recognized Valerie's writing voice, stylishly declarative, one staccato sentence after another, the short grafs going back to her summers interning at the *Philadelphia Inquirer.*

He was impressed that Valerie had gotten the piece to the Cut so quickly. Good for her. But even if Valerie was a fast writer, she wouldn't have written the essay just now. It read like something that had been worked on and reworked, maybe over years, maybe over years of bitter reflection. These days a lot of women were rethinking their past encounters with men, stewing over them. Valerie had been shrewd to light the fuse by going on record with a news organization first. The explosive response was what got her essay into the Cut.

Her journalistic shrewdness was maintained as she deftly led the reader from the general to the specific, from the challenges faced by all women reporters to the personal story of Valerie Iovine. Adam admired how she accomplished this, even as his anxiety built. The story she told about what happened in Max's office was precisely what she had told Adam at Metro Center, but with a fuller emotional response. She linked it to previous offenses against her as a woman and to the ones that lay ahead. These were not petty disappointments, Adam thought ruefully.

And then the retelling abruptly became chronological.

Uh-oh.

Valerie left Max's office. She walked unsteadily past her colleagues' cubicles. She went to the women's room to collect herself. She washed her face.

Adam thought he knew where this was going. The story was now like a cruise missile zeroing in on his home office. He could hear it whistle through the lower atmosphere. Around the twelve-hundred-word mark it should have come crashing through the ceiling.

But she wrote, "I then fled the building, dispirited and humiliated, to finish at home the article that I had been assigned. I still believed in the article, even if I had lost all confidence in my value as a journalist."

The papers on his desk remained in place. His desk was in one piece. He himself seemed to be intact. He checked his limbs. He listened to his body for reports of injury. All quiet.

She hadn't named him or referred to an unnamed colleague who was told about the incident. She could have named him or referred to him but she hadn't. Adam blushed as if he had been named.

He continued to read the piece, still anticipating his name, yet he was numbingly aware that she was passing over their encounter outside the women's restroom and her nearly immediate disclosure of what had happened in Max's office, the key corroboration of the editor's improper advance. This was a hole in the story a mile wide. She had never left holes in her stories like that. He reached the end of the article, where she painfully apologized that she had not come forward before now. She was distressed that her cowardice had allowed Max Lieberthol and other editors in the Washington media to keep preying on young women who had come to the capital to practice journalism.

He went back to the passage about leaving the restroom, as if he had simply missed the conversation at the Metro Center escalators. Had she *forgotten* the

Metro Center escalators? The embrace? Had she forgotten what happened just a few weeks later? Had she
forgotten *him*?

Logically thinking, he should have been relieved
now, and not only because he was excused for his silence
after his return to the office. But the thought that he had
been deleted from the narrative was rankling. He recalled
a single sentence in the piece they had worked on over the
phone that night. They had gone back and forth about the
placement of a long clause within it, and whether to set it
off with commas or em dashes, and that argument lasted
about five minutes, until they both started giggling. The
giggling went on for another minute. They both needed
that. This minute was as least as important as any other
minute of their time together.

Adam thought that Valerie's shrewdness had now
failed her. The absence of a third-party confirmation,
coupled with her twenty years' silence, was inevitably
noticed and discussed, drawing even further interest to
her piece, links to which were already being retweeted
left and right—the left because it cared about women in
the workplace, the right for the passing opportunity to
annihilate Max Lieberthol. The latter commenters, even
while chortling over Max's predicament, zealously cast
doubt on her credibility. They demanded to know why
she hadn't told anyone. But the left, too, was uneasy,
some tweets at least recognizing that the unsubstantiated

charge posed a mortal threat to a liberal institution, as imperfect as it was.

Had she no friends? Had she no colleagues at the magazine? How hostile an environment had it been? How hostile was it now? These questions were relevant to the larger #MeToo reckoning. Valerie had been let down not only by Max Lieberthol, one of the press corps' biggest big swinging dicks, *#UnsubscribeNDeal* observed that she had been let down by the men around him, an editorial power structure dominated by men. That this had happened at a progressive publication was all the more galling—and suggested that the magazine's progressive credentials should be reexamined. How many women had *ever* populated its staff box? How many people of color? Someone was probably doing the math right now.

Valerie hadn't named Adam, but the list of staff members at the magazine in the year 1999 was very limited. PDFs of old issues were online. You could easily make a list and now Adam saw that someone had, identifying every one of the former male writers and editors by their Twitter handles.

His notifications were skyrocketing. Fuck. He was being directly @'ed by people he didn't know. *Sexual harassment at the Next Deal. Did you witness it, @azweig?* Another: *@azweig, you must have known #Lieberlover was a letch. Why not report it?* Another: *@azweig, you've always stood with the patriarchy.* Another: *@azweig, can* *you confirm that she had nice tits?* And: *@azweig, please describe her breasts in full detail.* Other people, some of them journalists, female and male, were elaborating further about the old-boy culture at the magazine, where Adam hadn't been on staff since the George W. Bush administration.

Someone had excavated a style piece he wrote in 2002, about the robust, manly pleasures of a good cigar lounge. It hadn't worn well. The tweeter said Adam's insensitivity toward women had always been obvious.

Adam DocuSigned the MSNBC contract at once and sent it back. Then he closed the Twitter tab so he could think.

Fifteen seconds later, his phone lit up. The *Times*, finally.

How much willpower would be required not to answer a text from a reporter at the *New York Times*? Many years ago, barely out of his teens, hitchhiking through the Basque Country in rural Spain, Adam had stopped in a roadside bar to use the toilet, leaving his backpack at the counter. When he returned, the barman smiled and he felt obliged to order a beer. Adam had been traveling on a few pesos a day, trying to conserve the day's allowance for the next hostel. Lunch on the side of the road had been an apple and a piece of cheese. But the beer was delicious. The barman laid out the cold *pintxos* on a tray in front of him: sausage and peppers, bacon-wrapped dates, fried baby eels, and more. They were in shallow open dishes, piled high and skewered with toothpicks. Adam had already learned that *pintxos* weren't free like American bar snacks, and that whatever he took he would have to pay for, according to the number of toothpicks left on his plate. But now he was almost painfully hungry and he reminded himself how difficult this trip had turned out to be. He had no Spanish, the wait between rides was long, and he was lonely. The anchovies with olives and pickled green peppers seemed to mean more than a few salty calories. They represented the freedom and adventure for which he had come to Europe. He stared, no longer enjoying the beer. The fight to resist the *pintxos*, not to spend a few extra pesos, seemed consequential, not only for this trip, but also for the kind of person he was going to be. He held on. He paid for the beer and left. Not responding to a text from the *New York Times* would be something like that.

He couldn't go away from his desk long enough for a walk, not now, but he managed to leave his phone upstairs while he went out to the front yard. He stood on the short, expensively tended lawn for a few minutes. The day was still cool and the sound of traffic on another street, the cries of children playing, and the sky's transparency allowed him to imagine that this city was an ordinary place of ordinary pursuits. One of his neighbors drove by, the driver's window down. His name was Paul and Adam didn't know what he did, but presumably he was in the government, because he wasn't a journalist. The man smiled in what Adam thought was an inquisitive way, as if he, too, wanted to know about sexism at the *Next Deal* twenty years ago. The cell phone on Adam's desk tugged at him with invisible strings.

He climbed the stairs back to his office, where there was yet another text from the *Times*. The reporter was someone he didn't know. She must have been a new hire, someone in New York. She was asking him to call her. This was her third text.

He stared at the *gambas al ajillo* for a few moments, waiting for the screen to fade and go black. It seemed to be taking an extraordinarily long time to do so. He continued to watch it.

Then the phone popcorned. He swiped at it, answering the call without giving it another thought. Damn.

"Adam Zweig? It's Aurelie Dumesnil from the *New York Times*."

Now the byline seemed vaguely familiar, but she was certainly young. The reporters were getting younger all the time—the J-schools kept pumping them out. Her voice was rich and full-bodied, just a touch accented, possibly Europeanized. Adam wondered what Aurelie Dumesnil looked like.

He didn't apologize for not answering her texts. She didn't apologize for the cold call. She told him about the story in the Cut, summarizing it at some length, as if he wouldn't have already read it eight times. He patiently allowed her to do this. She then asked him if he was aware of the story.

Adam conceded that he knew about the story. This made him sound like he had been withholding the fact that he had read it. He felt as if he had been tricked, or at least wrong-footed. He had believed he was being polite.

"These charges are so out of the blue," she said. "And they have such consequence. People are wondering if there's any way they can be backed up. Right now it's just Valerie's word against Max's."

Adam made a show of shrugging, even though she couldn't see it. "You know, what happens between two people . . ."

"Very often other people learn of it. There may be witnesses. There may be confidences exchanged. People say you and Valerie were very, very close. Adam, she's getting attacked all over."

"What people are saying that?"

"From the magazine," Aurelie said vaguely.

He wondered whom she had talked to. He wondered how obvious his friendship with Valerie had been. He hadn't thought it was that obvious.

He said, with a show of indifference, "Yeah, that was common knowledge."

Aurelie said, "You were *friends*?"

Adam heard the emphasis. The emphasis meant that some people might have suggested he and Valerie were more than friends, or at least that their relationship occupied some category that lay beyond the conventional, sorely limited definitions of friendship.

He rushed to deny the suggestion. "Yes, we were friends. Friends and colleagues."

He heard the falseness in his literally true denial. He wondered what language could be made available to describe all the permutations of which human relationships were capable. The denial couldn't begin to describe their friendship and collegiality. Nor could it categorize what *did* happen, next. But he knew he was being false. Aurelie knew it too.

"She's getting slammed from all sides," the *Times* writer said. "And she's really on her own. She's a suburban reporter who hasn't worked in Washington for twenty years. She's not ready for this kind of media attention."

Aurelie couldn't see him redden, but she had confidently maneuvered him into a corner. The walls of the corner were uneven, their dimensions hard to gauge.

"I feel for her," he said feebly.

"Good friends," Aurelie insinuated. "I'm surprised she didn't tell you what happened between her and Max."

"She did," Adam blurted. "She did tell me."

On one level, he knew, he had stepped forward only to support Valerie, to defend her. This was the right thing to do. But once more he was aware that he could barely articulate his motives. The memory of the em dash argument had returned with force, in a flush of heat (they had finally agreed on commas). This heat impelled him to remind Valerie that he was part of the story. But he knew that he had also given into weakness. The narrative that he so much wanted to be part of led only to personal disaster.

Aurelie made no sound that indicated she knew she had just advanced the story.

"About how long after the incident?"

"Like fifteen minutes."

Now she made a little involuntary exhalation of surprise, not unfetchingly. You could hardly get more immediate than that. She asked him where and he described the top of the Metro Center escalators, being precise about which entrance they were at. He didn't tell the reporter about the embrace any more than he had told Luann.

"And what did she say happened?"

"Max made a pass. She told me everything that's in her story. Almost word for word."

He could hear her keyboard clicking emphatically with the unambiguous confirmation of Valerie's claim. Then Aurelie stopped.

"Wait. I don't understand. What were you doing at the Metro with her?"

Adam told her about meeting Valerie in the hallway after the incident, but not that he was waiting for her outside the bathroom. She was upset and he accompanied her from the building. He thought he sounded like a good guy.

"I see," Aurelie said.

The reporter was thinking this through. Adam wondered where she had come from before the *Times*, if she had started out at a second-string daily. What was her beat now? Was it the media or was it gender? It might make a difference in how she would write the story.

"She told you. And then what did you do?" Aurelie demanded.

He wanted to stay nonchalant, as if the question were innocent. "Oh you know, I went back to the office. I had an article to finish. I felt terrible for her of course. We talked on the phone later."

"Did you speak with Max?"

"About this? No."

"Why not?"

"Honestly, it didn't occur to me."

"But you were in a position of some power there, right?"

"I was a staff writer, that's all."

"'Writer and Editor,' according to the staff box. You had authority."

"Not really. Max ran the show. The staff would discuss stories, headlines, layout. That's it."

"But you could have done something."

"It wasn't clear what. I understood that she was deeply hurt. I also understood that Max had done something wrong. I was furious."

"You could have reported it."

"It was a small magazine. It wasn't like we had an HR department," Adam said, trying not to sound defensive, trying not to sound that he was aware that she was unsympathetic to him. He was trying to sound collegial, reporter-to-reporter, or perhaps avuncular. He was feeling his age now. She could have been thirty years younger than him. Trying to break the ice, and also because he was a total moron, Adam added, "Or a Special Victims Unit."

"I see," she said again.

The interview continued, now considerably chilled. She wanted to know whether Max had "propositioned" other women in the office. Adam said he didn't know. She asked whether Max had ever "flirted" with subordinates. Adam replied indistinctly. She circled several times around the "workplace situation." Was there a "culture of sexual intimidation," as Valerie claimed? Adam said it was a typical media office of the '90s, competitive and professional, but not always respectful. She demanded examples. He avoided giving her anything. He had given her enough by confirming Valerie's story.

She asked him when he had stopped being friends with Valerie. He said they stopped seeing each other once she stopped writing for the magazine. It had been only a work friendship, he said. There hadn't really been a personal element. Now he felt like Nixon declaring, "I am not a crook."

Aurelie had mostly stopped taking notes. She had already obtained what she needed for her story. When she finished asking questions, the conversation picked up speed, accelerated to the end, with one or two fewer sentences of thanks than one might have expected from a fellow professional.

LIFE IN A SHITSTORM. The precipitation was un-relenting. It fell from the skies in sheets. The winds could knock you over. Whatever could be said against you was elaborated, as if the original condemnation bumped against the limits of language, as if a new language, a new system of symbolic representation, had to be devised to get to the truth of your awfulness. And then it would be amplified on the social media that you followed and the social media that you'd never heard of, a brain-filling roar. The Special Victims Unit joke hadn't helped, of course. Aurelie had quoted it as something "Mr. Zweig said, seeming to make light of the incident."

The main point of the story, of course, was that Adam had verified Valerie's charge against Max. This ended the she-said, he-said stalemate. Adam was osten-sibly a hero, at least for those who read only the headline and the top three paragraphs. Some of these readers were lightning-like tweeters and a surge of praise momentarily flooded his feed. This felt good, momentarily.

But people quickly got past the first three grafs. His initial failure to bring Max to account was damning. His throwaway line halfway down the story only amplified the egregiousness. Now there was a "Next Deal: SVU"

meme. Adam had been uncaring. Adam had *protected*
Max. Everything Adam had ever written about women
was now picked over again, with even more scrutiny than
was exercised only a few hours earlier—on the Equal
Rights Amendment, on Hillary Clinton's 2008 primary
campaign—accompanied by wild surmises about his
"true" feelings about women (he wondered if some of
these surmises were correct). It was observed that he was
a divorced man, as if no one had been divorced before.
It was observed that he was *fifty-eight years old*. It was
observed that he was *white*. Opinion writers in both the
Times and the *Post* issued a blizzard of red-hot takes.

He wondered what Nuri Gelman thought. She had
never acknowledged receipt of the signed contract.

Adam had taken crap before, for controversial opinions, for predictions that proved wrong, and for simple
reporting mistakes. Those mistakes could pile up. This
felt different though. The crap-level was raised by at least a
factor or two. The amplitude made the criticism feel justi-
fied, even the criticism that he knew was objectively false.
The criticism reminded him, as if he needed reminding,
that there was still a hole in the public knowledge of the
story. It was the hole he would be buried in.

Jason called. "Dad, are you all right?"

Even with a four-word question, Jason was capable of
expressing sympathy and a wisdom beyond his years. He
was a rabbi, a Reconstructionist, the most liberal, politi-
cally engaged, and fresh thinking of the American Jewish

congregational types. As religiously nonconformist as he was, Jason was more religious than anyone in Adam's family going back several generations, back to another continent.

"I'm cool."

"But there's so much anger being directed at you. I recognize the lack of fairness. There was nothing you could have done then, given the time and place, given who you were at the time. I'm so sorry."

Given who I was? Adam was going to let that slide.

"If you don't go on the internet, it's fine," he said, as if that were a possibility.

And this wasn't even his shitstorm. It was a gust from someone else's shitstorm, a side breeze of a shitstorm, a little eddy of a shitstorm.

Nowadays, of course, you thought everything that happened was about you. Trump could be setting fire to the Constitution—he was—but it was your own ears that were burning, social media algorithms heightening the sentiment already embedded within human consciousness that every individual was at the center of the universe's attention. This was called a "referential delusion." Adam struggled to remember his insignificance. The universe didn't care that he was quoted in the *New York Times*. The Max and Valerie story wasn't about him. It was about Max and Valerie.

This was proven correct when he went back to his feed. Another barrage was coming in—but the target was Max, and the ammunition against the "progressive predator" was hyperbolically vituperative. *Politico* was running an update. It led with Adam's support of Valerie's claim, of course, but then it went on to rehash Max's previous run-ins with conventional liberal opinion, including arguments over urban gentrification and campaign finance. The magazine had also supported, for human rights principles, the 2003 invasion of Iraq. Other websites offered their own takes, but the main judgment was that Max was a dinosaur and the asteroid had been long due.

Adam wondered if Max would really withstand this now that the main news outlets had taken on the story. The name Max Lieberthol had once meant something, the definition of a certain kind of American liberalism. Now it was coming to mean something else, something still unsettled, but it wouldn't be good. You would think, looking at social media, that being an editor of a little-read policy-focused political magazine made him a pillar of the patriarchy. But as long as he held that position, he would remain a strategic object. Would he know how to walk away? Would he know how to salvage something of his reputation?

No, probably not. He wouldn't leave. If anything, the old man would think, in error, that this fight would re-energize him, just as other fights had. He would engage his critics at the battlements, pike in hand. He would bring down the magazine with him.

So it would be up to the finance guys. They had been named in the *Politico* story, almost in passing, since it was so hard to think of the *Next Deal* as anything but Max's magazine. Damon Brosseau and Silas Arbuthnot. Adam had once met Arbuthnot at a Democratic fundraiser. He was a mid-level donor, modest and personable, reasonably well-informed, and young enough to be a member of the generation that thought the most pressing issue faced by the republic was marijuana legalization. Since he and Brosseau purchased the magazine, the *Next Deal* had in fact done several good pieces about drug sentencing inequalities, but Max had probably not needed the encouragement.

Adam now recalled that he had also once talked to Brosseau. It had been about a year or so before the men bought the *Next Deal*, a weird conversation, a phone interview for a general interest story about market-disrupting advances in high-frequency trading. The guy, a quantitative analyst, was enthusiastic about his small, lucrative contribution to the science of stochastic calculus. Adam had never heard of stochastic calculus and Brosseau had never heard of *The Atlantic*, so they were even. Oddly—but Adam had expected the conversation to go oddly—Brosseau behaved as if this were a social call and he asked Adam cocktail party questions like how many kids he had. He showed a conspicuous lack of interest in the answers. He didn't care at all about the article that Adam was writing. But when Brosseau asked what Adam did for fun, he expressed genuine curiosity about Adam's indifferently maintained fantasy baseball team. "Corey Kluber? Really?" In the end, Adam understood enough about the newly developed technology to write a two-thousand-word article about how it would transform certain kinds of stock market investment, but not enough, sadly, for him to do anything with his 401(k).

No demands for Max's dismissal had been directed at the guys yet, as far as Adam could see. But the demands would come. They'd have to make the decision. Max would go to war against them, too, of course.

WITH SOME EFFORT, Adam continued to ignore further texts, emails, and tweets, but when Max's name lit up his phone—three letters: *Max*—he stared at it as if it were an impossible combination of alphanumeric characters. *Max.* The last time he and Max spoke had been nearly a year ago, when Max had some last-minute questions about his midterms piece. He slid open the call reflexively, again.

"You prick."

"Nice to hear from you, Max."

"You cretinous, mendacious, sneaking, snuffling, self-dramatizing poseur."

"I told the truth."

"Why didn't you tell me *then* she had a complaint?"

"I thought it was something personal."

"It was! It was entirely between us, you should have never been involved. But once you were, you could have warned me."

Adam heard something beneath the vibratos of anger in Max's voice, which he was accustomed to hearing in his voice anyway, the more righteous the better. Adam didn't hear righteousness now. He wondered if he was hearing regret, or fear, or if he was only projecting what would have been his own feelings.

"I didn't know what to do, Max."

"Yeah. I bet you didn't."

Uncomfortably aware of a vague accusation, Adam said, "She was very upset."

"It's maddening. Someone makes a claim against you and there's no way to defend yourself, no matter how outlandish the charge is. The other person can make it up from scratch. They may have never even *met* you, but, you know, people say, well, maybe, if she's making a claim, she must have a reason. Adam, it's McCarthyism all over again."

Adam was silent for a few moments. He wondered why he had always been quick to take Max's call.

"Why not say I did the Brink's robbery? Why not say I killed Kennedy?" Max declared, "I'm going to fight this."

"Max," Adam began.

"What?"

"Max," Adam repeated. He sighed. "Are you saying you never *met* her?"

"Don't be a child."

"Are you saying you didn't make a pass?"

Max made a sound of disgust that was probably accompanied by a furious scowl.

"'A pass.' That's one thing you can call it. Adam, I asked Valerie Iovine for a date. She was single. I was single. I was attracted to her. I had the temerity to believe she could be attracted to me. It was a romantic overture. It was sloppy, I admit, but since when is that sexual harassment? Sloppy romantic overtures are how men and women have come together from the beginning of time up to last Saturday night. Sunday morning. Very often there's a misunderstanding about mutual interest, the overture's rebuffed, and life goes on. The misunderstanding isn't brought up twenty years later as proof of turpitude. Or worse."

"Max, you were her editor. She was a freelance writer who needed a job. It wasn't an even playing field."

"I guarantee you, Adam, no one ever makes love on an even playing field. We always bring one inequality or another into the relationship. One lover will always have more money than the other, or more professional power, or better looks, or higher societal status, or youth. Think of someone with whom you've been involved in which that wasn't the case. One individual never has the same attributes as another, which is why we *need* the other."

"You told her she had 'lovely' breasts."

The editor missed a beat here, uncharacteristically. It was all over social media, but he was shamed now that Adam had brought it up. Both men knew that Max Lieberthol, who had won the Pulitzer Prize for Commentary, would be forever famous for that remark.

"They were nice," Max conceded, trying to recover his composure, and Adam heard him allow some wistfulness into the comment. This sparked in Adam some wistfulness of his own. He never forgot what he saw, the single time. He never forgot their weight in his hands, that other time, later. "All right, that was a coarse remark. Pillory me for making a coarse remark in the previous century. When I look back at a long, eventful life, I regret many things. This is one of the least of them."

"Don't be so sure, Max. They want your head out there."

"In expressing my feelings for Valerie, I was in no way offering any sort of quid pro quo. She doesn't claim I did, if you read that nearly illiterate philippic carefully."

Adam tried to interrupt. "Her writing's good—"

"But that's what the fake-feminist #MeTooers are saying. It's profoundly dispiriting. It's as if everything I fought for in my career, for the rights and for the humanity of the individual, means nothing to them. But that's the problem with their half-baked crusade. They don't believe that a romantic relationship can be anything but transactional."

"Are you going to apologize?"

"No!" he said, as if Adam were out of his mind. "No fucking way. I've been in this town long enough.

People know what I've done for the cause of women and for individual women journalists. The articles we reported—about equal pay, about sex workers, about women's health—all testify to my deep commitment to the welfare of women. This work is far more important to the magazine's legacy than a sentimental initiative upon which I clumsily embarked on a single occasion."

Max paused for a moment, to slow himself down. Adam could feel the heat coming through the phone.

The editor said, "That's why I'm humbly asking the significant writers and political thinkers of our time to come to my aid."

Adam smiled at the word *humbly*.

Max named five luminaries, men and women, each ranking slightly higher than Adam. It was a very impressive list.

"And now I'm turning to you, Adam. I'm not passing around a petition. I admire you too much as a writer and a thinker to ask you to put your name to anything you haven't written yourself. Nor am I asking you to speak of anything private involving Valerie, or for you to write about her at all. But I feel I can fairly ask you to help me clear my good name, to write a letter to the *New York Times* attesting to my decency, my probity, and my compassion and respect for other people. Would you do that?"

Adam silently noted that Max didn't confirm the five luminaries were actually writing letters. He also reminded himself that Max had begun this conversation by calling him a prick, etc. The third thing he was forced to acknowledge was that he still believed in Max's decency, probity, and compassion and respect for other people.

"Jeez, Max. I'm already on the record confirming Valerie's claim."

"This will make your letter even stronger," he insisted. "And Valerie's claim is *specious*."

"I'm going to have to think about exactly what I would say."

Max heard Adam's evasiveness.

The editor blurted, "You know, she's out for vengeance. She's crazy. She thinks this is going to make up for every personal and professional setback she's ever come up against."

Adam heard Max's bitterness. This was a sign of his advanced age, his inability to hold back. A younger man would have known not to attack the woman. A younger man would have responded to Adam's evasiveness with at least faked understanding.

Adam said, "C'mon, Max. You *know* women have it tougher in this business. You *know* it's unfair. So, naturally, now they're angry."

"I'd worry about it if I were you. You were far worse than I was. You think I don't know what you were up to with her? Those afternoons out of the office? I was at least an unmarried man."

"You're so goddamn out of line, Max."

"She's trying to destroy me!" the editor suddenly cried, in a voice Adam never heard before. It was almost womanish. "She's trying to destroy the magazine. This is not something I built myself. You built it. Quentin Harper and Charlotte Skinner built it. Our readers built it. The *Next Deal* is a *movement* that's outlasted five administrations. Now Valerie Iovine and the #MeTooers are going to kill it over some bullshit triviality."

"You're wrong about me and Valerie. I was helping her with a story. We weren't doing anything."

Max didn't speak for a moment, but a tremor in his breathing manifested his pain, how he was being buffeted by the whirlwind of public reprobation and humiliation. It was a whirlwind of a shitstorm, a tornado. The man was on his knees, so lost that he could barely see.

Max finally said, "Yeah, right."

This was the seventh time that one of the men told the other man to go fuck himself.

ADAM PACED his home office, a distance of two steps one way and then two steps back, sweating heavily. He was hardly agitated by the editor's anger. No, it was his blind, wild shot through Adam's curtain of decency and self-control. Once more, as if it were really necessary, Adam had shown himself to be absolutely visible, absolutely transparent. Everyone saw him. As a man, it was as if he had spent his entire adult life walking around without pants or underwear. No, going back to adolescence. As if, with just a glance, *ewww*, everyone had always known what was on his mind. Was it the one thing on his mind? Was *that* what it meant to be a man?

Valerie's ocean story had made that month's next cover, her first. The cover art wasn't good, centered around a muddy picture of fishermen in slickers—what was that supposed to be?—but Valerie was exhilarated. Inside the issue the story ran eight pages, with sharp graphics drawn from the NOAA and UN data. Rereading the story for about the seventeenth time, Adam was jolted. This was serious. The rise in ocean temperatures was an existential threat to human civilization.

They celebrated with lunch at Chi-Chi's in an office building near the National Archives. Valerie had changed for the occasion. She was wearing black slacks that he had never seen before and what was possibly a new blouse with a cute French ruffle in the front. She had done something with her hair that he couldn't have begun to describe. Predictably for a guy, he hadn't changed. They ordered margaritas.

He couldn't remember now what they had eaten or talked about at lunch twenty years ago, not after what happened next. The story? Future stories, too, probably. She had developed excellent sources at the National Oceanographic and Atmospheric Administration. What he would most want to remember from that lunch was her effervescence, how her speech bubbled out of her, and how those bubbles seemed to enter his own bloodstream. She had plenty to tell him, apparently. She couldn't stop talking, he recalled. She made her points with her fork in the air. Her eyes glittered, as if Chi-Chi's had disco lights overhead. His eyes must have glittered too. He was taking in the whole of her across the table: her youth, her enthusiasm, her warmth, something more than warmth.

The lunch itself receded down a dim, salsa-tinted corridor of memory, but all these years later Adam was warmed again by that sensation, her unmistakable affection for him. Those were bubbles of affection that had entered his bloodstream, barely macroscopic indicators that someone cared for him. Yes, let's call it desire—that's what he had seen in her eyes, and that was all anyone could ever hope for. All the nonsense that fed the culture and with which we surrounded ourselves, all the boy-girl nonsense in the office: the flirting, the postures, the pretensions, the provocations, heels, macho muscle, Skinner's jokes, Max's bumblings, the singles' tentative sparring that circled around the question of a date. It all came down to wanting to be wanted. He believed then, across the table, that something was being confirmed.

The next thing he remembered was that they had left Chi-Chi's. They were in the passage to the building's elevators outside the restaurant's doors, both still lifted by the same buoyancy they had shared over lunch. Valerie was laughing at her own happiness. Office workers swirled around them. Adam had to get back to the magazine for a meeting.

What happened next may have been brought about by nothing less banal than the mix-made margaritas. Adam and Valerie stood opposite each other in the passage, Valerie's face flushed, her eyes moist, no longer glittering. He knew his own face had turned red. They stopped smiling. They waited a long, unsmiling moment.

He would never be sure who initiated this, no matter how many times he reran it in his mind. No matter how much he had wanted it to happen. Their lips first touched gently. The touch was a shock. It became a long kiss and people continued to pass around them as they had at the top of the Metro pit, and they were maybe even the same people. It was a popular Chi-Chi's. He felt her body press against him again, with even more force than the afternoon several weeks earlier. And it was just as true that his body was making the effort, generated by his own need.

They pulled back, still holding each other and holding on to the moment too.

He was trembling, and not only from desire. He may have been as frightened as he had been in Mogadishu when he saw the helicopters go down.

He moved toward her lips again, and she turned perhaps an eighth of an inch away.

But she came back and kissed him again, now full on the lips, fully in his embrace, and he felt her heat. Not unclenching, they shuffled a few feet down the hall to get out of the way of people leaving the restaurant.

They broke for a moment, he kissed the side of her neck, and he felt something rise up within her.

Here was a single-occupancy public restroom. Adam had used it once on the way to an interview. He was astonished that he could have possibly remembered it. He reached down and turned the knob.

"No, Adam."

"Yes," he said, not recognizing the voice of his choked, low-pitched insistence.

"No, Adam. Not now."

"Yes now. Now now now."

"No."

"Yes."

"No."

"Yes."

"You're out of your mind," she whispered.

He told himself the statement was delivered with at least a measure of admiration.

She allowed him to lead her into the restroom or, rather, they were still embracing, so some pressure had to be applied, and it could not be said that there was no resistance. The force of his arms on her shoulders was slightly more than was necessary for guidance. One might compare it to, say, making a turn without power steering. The opposing force was less than enough to provide an impediment. One might compare it to, say, the resistance from a turnstile or a drawer that had come off its tracks. Even in the moment, Adam couldn't calculate precisely the material impulses at work.

He thought it was better not to turn on the light, but when the door banged shut behind them the restroom fell into a profound darkness, so dark it was dangerous. He couldn't possibly remember the layout of the fixtures or even where the lock on the door was. It took him a few moments of fumbling to find the switch.

The light came on like an atomic explosion, scorching their eyes to the back of their optic nerves, and they were both startled by what the light revealed, as if they had never been in a public restroom before. The restroom wasn't filthy, but it wasn't clean either. The slate floor was worn and spotty. Streaks of congealed pink soap lined the wet sink. Used brown paper towels were scattered about, rustling in the breeze generated by the fan that had started up with the light. The restroom contained a toilet stall and a urinal. In the latter, some gray chewing gum rested on a tattered mat. A disinfectant smell overpowered whatever was the scent of Valerie's lip gloss. The other revelation was that they were both there. Sorry to touch the doorknob again, Adam made sure the button was pushed in.

He placed his hands on her shoulders and they kissed once more.

"Are you serious?" she said.

The question seemed to have levels upon levels to it. One of the levels comprised nothing but this moment.

The others, connected by hidden, Escheresque stair-cases, contained branching and intersecting corridors of multiple destinies, dead-end hallways, homey rooms with fireplaces and plate glass windows opening onto nebulous vistas, and some with neither windows nor doors.

Her lips were soft. The fan was loud.

He turned her around and put his lips on her neck again, knowing he had found the right spot. He gently reached for her breasts, which, as he had guessed during lunch, were taking an unbrassiered day. He was now surprised by their weight or, rather, by the *reality* of their presence beneath his hands. She made a breathy, vocal sound, possibly indicating something like pleasure. She unbuttoned her slacks and pulled them a half inch down her hips, tentatively, not ready to lower them further, not sure where this was really going. He bent over to shimmy the pants and her underwear down below her knees, kissing the inside of her knees and the back of her legs on his return up. He dropped his own pants and boxers. Leaning over the sink, resting her hands on it, she made that sound again, not quite a moan. Maybe it was on the way to a moan.

The bathroom wasn't sexy, but it *was* sexy, in a desperate, need-to-do-it-now, down and dirty kind of way with which Adam had no experience. In these several minutes he and Valerie weren't two Washington magazine writers, one of them hurtling toward middle age, in a single-occupancy public restroom outside the doors

to a Chi-Chi's restaurant, but maybe, like, what? Rock
stars? Drug addicts? College students? Thank God
there was no mirror above the sink. Thank God there
was no mirror in the restroom.

They both seemed surprised when he slid inside
and of course he wasn't wearing a condom, the absence
of which he knew was the height of irresponsibility, the
summit of a mountain of irresponsibility, but this afternoon's post-lunch appointment hadn't been on his cal-
endar, not today or ever. He had entered a new place,
not exactly like any other place he had been before. And
now her vocalization could be identified as an almost
definitive moan, a Valerie Iovine–specific sound that, no
matter how well he would have come to know her, no
matter how close their friendship would have become,
he would have never had the privilege of hearing if he
had not been with her right now, holding her hips, in
this restroom.

He pulled up on her hips and thought he felt something respond within her core. Her head was bent over
the sink. He thrust forward and she may have thrust
back, trying to get the rhythm. As they moved, together
and at odds, he was acutely aware of himself, his physical self, and of what Valerie and his physical self were
doing—*We're fucking!*—and that this was where their
friendship and their collaboration and their urgent
needs had brought them. He knew that this was exactly
what he had wanted all the time. He also knew that this

was what *Max* had wanted for himself, Max, the avatar of progressive political journalism, the professional he most looked up to and was most often at loggerheads with. He was reminded that Max had been a party to all this. He might as well have been there. Then Adam tried to drive down again.

Yet another person was in the bathroom, sitting behind the toilet stall's half-open door on the closed seat, smirking. That would be Luann. What had *happened* with him and Luann, anyway? When exactly had she drifted away into the deepest, most mephitic bowels of the American criminal justice system? When did her life become so heroic, and his so petty? She was looking at him more intensely than usual, but the attention was cold and contemptuous. She was worse than a mirror. Adam turned away.

The height of the restroom sink wasn't quite standard, at least not for this. Valerie was a little too stooped, and he was coming in a little too high, and every time they reached a rhythm together they lost it, and they had to start again. He slightly shifted his position. So did she. They started again.

There were just so many times you could do that. Actually, two and a half times.

"Uh-oh," he said. "Uh-oh," he said again. "Whoops."

"Fuck."

"Sorry."

She groaned, and not in pleasure.

Damn. Damn. Damn. Damn.

He tried to resume. He couldn't. He pulled away, startled by the mess he had created, and was still creating, on her slacks and on her legs, and on his beige Dockers, too, a remarkable volume for a thirty-eight-year-old man. The floor.

She turned slowly. Her face had taken on a look of resignation. It might have been shading toward anger. He re-embraced her. Her kiss was still soft at least.

"Jesus, Adam," she said. He detected some tenderness. "That was *terrible.*"

"I know," he said, gravely embarrassed. Once he thought about it, repeatedly, over the moments, days, and decades to follow, he'd be chagrined, every time from a place of deeper mortification. From a mechanical point of view, it had been a total fiasco. But right now it didn't feel *exactly* like a fiasco, he thought. Something had been accomplished. They had accomplished it together, not without struggle. Some new thing was being started. But it was still embarrassing.

His pants still bunched down by his feet, he hopped over to the paper towel dispenser, which, *Baruch HaShem,* by the mercy of a benevolent God and Chi-Chi's, too, was full, though so full it was overstuffed. He had to yank out the sheets. They initially came out in torn scraps, adding to the debris on the floor. Public restrooms were really as bad as you thought they were.

He handed her a stack of full sheets. Her face was flushed.

"Oh Jesus, Adam," she said.

She dabbed at her slacks. He pulled up his pants and wiped the floor with extra care. He washed his hands vigorously.

She allowed him to kiss her again, but just barely.

"Let's go back," he murmured, meaning her apartment.

"This was a mistake," she said slowly.

"Mistakes were made," he said, as was often said in the nation's capital. "But it wasn't a mistake."

A wan, possibly painful smile might have been coming to her lips. She was confused and undecided. She said tentatively, "OK. At least to talk. About this. About what's going on."

"More than talk," he said ardently.

"Let's talk. In my experience, you know how to talk. The other thing . . ."

"Wait," he said. "No, I can't. I have an editorial meeting."

She already knew about the meeting, but she seemed surprised, especially after she had just agreed to let him come back. Still holding him, she looked into his face as if searching in its crannies and pores for the real reason he had changed his mind.

"We have a Fed story next issue," he said. "If I'm not there, they're going to put Alan Greenspan on the cover."

Whatever was left to cool cooled in her eyes. That was why you didn't put Alan Greenspan on the cover. He kissed her again.

He said, "I'll be finished by four."

FOR A LONG TIME, Adam had thought there was some significance in Valerie Iovine not being on LinkedIn. He had looked for her there, as he had looked on all the social media for the accounts of every woman with whom he had ever shared any kind of friendship, attachment, or romance. Where had they gone, what were they doing, were they married, did they have kids? This search seemed perfectly normal. He never tried hard enough to approach anything like cyber-stalking, but it wasn't like he didn't think of Valerie somewhat more often than from time to time. She wasn't on Facebook either. He knew, though, that she worked for the *Virginian-Pilot*.

Her Twitter account was strictly professional: links to her stories in the paper and the occasional dutiful retweet of a colleague's. Her Twitter bio read simply, "Features at the Pilot. She/her." There was no picture. He had begun following her years ago.

Even now she was linking only to the Cut essay, not to any of the news accounts of her charge against Max Lieberthol and not to anything about Max ricocheting around the internet. Nor was she tweeting about the incident further.

The modesty of her social media presence was alien to Adam's experience as a journalist. A reporter's job was to get the news out, by every means available. You had to go on cable or NPR if they asked, and you fervently hoped they would. Your continued comments about the issues you covered, on Twitter and elsewhere, was follow-up reporting. Valerie's limited Twitter activity was weak professionalism. But not being on LinkedIn or Facebook was something like hiding.

From what? Adam was forced to acknowledge that whatever had happened to her twenty years ago, *everything* that had happened to her, had made her want to leave Washington. To flee. And then to stay off social media.

And what had inspired her to resurface now? #MeToo, of course. Me *too*: the emphatic confirmation that the humiliations, debasements, and the physical and nonphysical harassments she had suffered were not hers alone. Other women were reporting that they had shared them. Of course they had. We knew it all the time, men and women, for millennia. These indignities had been accepted as a fact of human existence, a fact of life on a planet ruled by men. Violence had initially brought the men to power. It could still be exercised. Women were reminding themselves—*themselves*, that's what this was about—that this power wasn't a physical principle like entropy or gravity, or a moral one. They could at least *disagree* with it. They could at least wonder how their lives had been shaped by it. Valerie had probably been brooding about what happened with Max for years. Until #MeToo, she may not have understood the *meaning* of it. Of course she would have recalled what happened with Adam as well.

Women were also thinking, speculating, wishing, dreaming that they could hold men accountable.

Now that Adam was looking in earnest, Valerie Iovine's personal information was easy enough to find. Only a few extra keystrokes opened the Yale alumni newsletter and an obscure City of Norfolk database. Googling, he came up with some creative search terms to accompany her name. Now it felt a little like cyber-stalking, but still nothing too weird. As soon as her name had shown up in the original *Politico* story, other people would have started deep-googling too.

She was unmarried, he discovered, disappointed. Although long divorced, Adam still regarded marriage as the proper adult condition. She had *never* been married. *Hmm*. She was living in a rental. She drove a 2012 gray Prius that had been bought used. She maintained her membership in the Society of Professional Journalists, which she had joined as an undergraduate. Also, the Chrysler Museum of Art in Norfolk, the Richmond Ballet, and the Virginia Museum of Fine Arts, but no advocacy organizations. She was being journalistically scrupulous about avoiding even a remote conflict of interest. She had also avoided involvements with the law—except, wait, a long-standing Freedom of Information request to the

Virginia Department of State Police. Yeah, good luck with that.

She had done excellent work for the *Pilot*, many environmental stories, some politics, a lot of in-depth features. Adam thought she was probably the *Pilot*'s best writer, but he found no indication that they considered her a star. She kept a low profile everywhere, including at the paper.

Clicking backward through the years, he saw that she had started out at the *Pilot* in 2009 doing cop checks, the same tasks she had performed as a summer intern for the *Philadelphia Inquirer* in the mid-1990s. She must have hated that. Before then she had freelanced, mostly in the Philadelphia and Delaware Valley regions, mostly for small, local publications, most of them no longer extant. Then, descending through the early years of the century, Adam encountered a conspicuous gap in her publication history. She had done her last *Next Deal* piece in 1999. Her byline wasn't seen again anywhere until 2005.

Huh. That was a long time to have not been writing.

Adam went back to her last several stories in the *Next Deal*. She had been cooking on all burners that year. He reread the ocean-warming story that he had helped her with, shocked again by its urgency and now by its prescience. The piece was a triumph of science reporting, patiently told with color and verve. But as she exited the office building where the Chi-Chi's was located, her slacks soiled, sticky, and wet, the story wouldn't have felt like a triumph at all.

He scrolled and clicked, ignoring everything else popping up on his screen.

Sometime early in the summer of 1999 (as Adam imagined it, piecing things together from the online scraps), Valerie had loaded up her car, license 803-648, "No Taxation Without Representation," and embraced her roommate on the street. The roommate, a little bewildered, was holding a check for the three months of rent still left on their lease. She watched Valerie drive away. Valerie would have made a left on Connecticut and taken that to Chevy Chase, where she would have gotten onto I-495N.

Valerie had told her parents only the night before that she was coming home. She would stay with them just one week, she declared. They said they would be delighted. But they were alarmed. They knew something had happened. They might have guessed it involved a man. Not that they would ever ask.

Valerie left the radio off as she drove north. She was allowing her many emotions to swirl through her that morning, undiluted by music or news. She didn't want anything to keep her from fully experiencing the sense of failure that she had won the right to feel. These emotions were mostly adjacent to sorrow. DC had been a bust and a half.

Fortunately, her mother and father had turned her bedroom into some kind of sewing room, so Valerie didn't have to reoccupy the memory zone of her childhood misfortunes, whatever they were. Her parents had made other changes to the house at 1906 Gladstone Street as well, including the addition of a new living room wall unit, yet everything about the house was still home, for good and bad. She slept in the guest room, trying to imagine that she had gone somewhere entirely new, possibly foreign.

When Valerie left the house to run errands, she hurried off the street so that she wouldn't have to talk to the immediate neighbors (Donna Franzoni, Angela Delrosso), but they knew she was back. So sad, such a bright, pretty girl. Went to Yale! Valerie made no attempt to connect with friends from Masterman High School.

Adam didn't think that Valerie was self-dramatizing enough to abandon in Washington the copies of the *Next Deal* to which she had contributed, but she kept them in a sealed cardboard box. Her parents were usually at work when new issues of the magazine arrived through their mail slot. She put those directly into recycling. Her parents didn't miss them nor any of the remaining issues of their subscription. For the sake of consistency, she should have also disposed of the magazine's increasingly importunate pleas to resubscribe, every one of them authored by Max Lieberthol, editor in chief—but that seemed like a never-ending project or overneurotic, an unhealthy overcommitment to her unhappiness. She let the letters pile up with the other junk mail. Anyway, her parents never resubscribed.

She could have applied to the *Inquirer* for a job, her editors were still there, but she hardly thought to do so (Adam continued to guess). Her summer internships were starting to look, in retrospect, like a big nothing. She had been a peppy young girl then, with a ponytail. They had seen her as a peppy young girl, assigning her to call the cops, cover night meetings, and chase trivial details for other reporters' stories, details that rarely reached print. They once sent her down to the Shore to report on a sandcastle-building contest and that hadn't made the paper either. Now, instead, through Yale's career placement office, she found a job working as a vocational guidance counselor serving immigrant high school students in Manayunk. The wages were low and she continued to live with her parents for another six months, to their increasing concern.

The following winter Valerie went back to school, going for a degree in social work from Drexel. *Drexel?* Penn had a School of Social Work. Adam thought the Ivy League graduate's choice of Drexel, rather than Penn, signified ambivalence and despair, though it could have simply been a matter of finances. She continued to work for the vocational guidance agency, rising through the hierarchy slowly, as if against her will. She liked the kids at least. She shared an apartment in Mount Airy with another woman.

Had she dated? Adam had no way of finding that out, not without *really* deep-googling. She would have been in her late twenties and early thirties. He assumed she dated, but gingerly. She was still trying to figure out what had happened with Josef; Josef was the big mystery looming over her life. She didn't want to make that mistake again, if she could figure out what that mistake was. Then there was the thing with Max—not *her* mistake, she resolved to believe, but he was still lording it over Washington, still posing as the great champion of women's rights. Him she hated. She kept on replaying in her mind the encounter in his office. The humiliation was the same, but now it was compounded by regrets about what she could have said in response, what she could have done. She believed that there was a correct combination of words that would have put Max in his place if she'd had only the wit and courage to summon them. Words that would have punished him and kept her in Washington. An incantation. So, again, she believed that she had somehow misplayed the situation.

And then . . . and then there was Adam. That loser. Another phony. Really a trivial piece of shit. No fucking mystery there. She had been an idiot to think he was her friend.

All three men, though, were bundled together in her experience of her twenty-sixth year. Try to pull one out and the other two came with him, grabbing hold of an arm or a leg, followed by other men or fragments of men or thoughts of men or desires of men, past and future.

No, Adam recognized, or at least suspected, that his imagination was failing him here. Valerie may have thought he was *more* than a loser and a phony, or a *more*-than-trivial piece of shit, *not* indistinguishable from the other two men. He may have recognized or suspected this or felt it like something indigestible in his gut for two decades now.

She had meanwhile, sometime early in the 2000s, discovered that she had made yet *another* mistake. She didn't really care for social work. What had she been thinking? What had she talked herself into? There was no end to the life-navigation mistakes you could make in your twenties.

She eventually, with some prodding by a friend, sent out to a few big-city newspapers her résumé and clips, including her *Next Deal* clips, including the ocean-warming story. They were good clips, plus she was a Yale graduate, but she hadn't produced a byline in several years, and her approaches to the *Globe*, to the *Times-Picayune*, to the *Chronicle*, to the *Plain Dealer*, and to the *Journal-Constitution* were tentative shots in the dark. After a few rejections or nonresponses, she abandoned the effort.

Valerie kept her job, but she started freelancing for local Philadelphia and suburban publications, including the *Inquirer*'s arts section. They hardly paid; this was mostly a hobby, really. She couldn't tell you why she was doing these stories about community groups, local artists, and neighborhood cleanup efforts—except, as she did them, she was rediscovering how much she liked making the first call, conducting the interview, and writing up the piece. And how *well* she did it. And how much she liked being in print or up on a website. Her dissatisfaction with social work intensified.

The resumed job search was more intense, her letters targeted to specific editors. This time she made follow-up calls, often more than one. She knew she had to pursue the job in a *certain* aggressive way; not *other* aggressive ways. The proper aggressive way for her was probably different from what would be favored in an applicant who was a man. Every rejection felt like a criticism, but she pushed on. She took off from work for several in-person interviews, in Reading, Hartford, and Somerset, New Jersey, and in Middletown, New York. She had insisted on these interviews. When the jobs didn't pan out, she wondered if the editors thought she wasn't pretty enough or what.

The offer from the *Pilot* came after three interviews, the editors around the table gazing at her with unblinking suspicion. She was warned the hiring was provisional. Her first performance review would be in a month. They were starting her out on cop checks. The pay was absurd, less than she had been making with the nonprofit. She accepted without hesitation. She rented an apartment in the Olde Towne section of Portsmouth.

As a matter of professional pride, journalists always complained about their crappy jobs and their bungling editors, but Valerie, once she started at the paper, kept her complaints to herself. She also kept to herself her plentiful satisfactions—the day in, day out news gathering, the stories themselves, the newsroom hustle, the sociability of her coworkers (none of whom she dated), the rush of the deadline, and the simple miracle of a new paper being turned out from scratch every day. She worked diligently, with covert self-confidence. She had now been at the *Pilot* ten years.

A recent video surfaced, from a public panel convened at UVA a few months ago to discuss local coverage of the 2018 midterm elections. In the clip, three women reporters occupied the stage. Adam required a moment to pick out the one who was Valerie Iovine. She had gained weight around the shoulders. Also: jowls and a grayish pallor. And her hair was still brown black, but not the same brown black that he remembered. He reflected, damning himself for the thought, but not without a tiny flush of satisfaction—*What a scumbag*—that from twenty-six to forty-six was a long way for a woman, further than from thirty-eight to fifty-eight was for a man. She probably never left the house these days without a bra.

And then whatever was different about Valerie abruptly vanished. There she *was*, in that two-month-old video. He could no longer recall what she looked like in 1999. But he remembered the thin careful smile, which was still there, as she spoke about the DS200 optical scan voting machines installed by the City of Norfolk. The machines generated paper ballots and were ADA compliant. The voice was intimately familiar. So was the South

Philly accent. She was telling *him* about the audit procedure. The commonwealth mandated a "risk-limiting audit," which statistically determined the possible margin of error and degree of confidence in the results. For example, in the District 13 House of Delegates race in 2017, the Department of Elections determined the winner with a confidence of 99.715 percent. He felt the old stirring.

AFTER CHI-CHI'S and a lightning strike at Banana Republic, Adam had returned to the office in a state of mind that could generally be described as distracted. His mental state was also elevated, expectant, aroused, confused, and anxious. And he probably reeked of semen, even in his new chinos. He forgot to look at his cell phone. The meeting dragged on, Adam trying to force his way through his funk to explain why the Fed was the wrong cover story for the next issue. The next interest rate hike would be minimal, consistent with recent policy. The magazine had run Greenspan in 1997. In the end, the best he could do was persuade Max to make Greenspan share the cover with a woman, his wife, the television journalist Andrea Mitchell.

It wasn't until he returned to his cubicle that he unfolded his cell and saw that he had missed a call from Luann, followed by three calls from Jason, who would have just walked in from school. The calls had come one right after another. Alarmed, Adam immediately phoned home.

"Hey, you OK?"

"Did you talk to Mom?"

"Not yet, I was in a meeting. Is she OK?"

"She's super upset. I can't believe you didn't call her."

"I was worried about *you*. What happened?"

"She lost all her appeals. Every single one. The Supreme Court refused a stay. The governor declared that there would be no commutation. Mom was beside herself. She said she failed Hobart. She said she called you at the office and on your cell. Dad, she was *crying*!"

The boy was frightened. He had managed to get this far in life without having to bear witness to displays of emotional distress from his parents.

"She worked very hard on the case. I'll call her now."

"They're putting him to death tomorrow morning!" Jason exclaimed. The execution had been delayed so many times Adam had forgotten that the date was coming up. "It's so backward. Hobart's a real person, with a real life story and real feelings. I feel like I *know* him. And they're going to kill him!"

Luann didn't pick up on her cell. Adam left a message and tried one of her cocounsels. She said Luann was at the penitentiary with Hobart, but she would tell her he called. The woman was in a hurry to get off, she was taking a flurry of media calls. Adam checked what was being reported online. The AP had a quote from the governor, who said that before declining the commutation he had prayed for guidance. He had gone down to his knees. Adam called Jason once more. The boy hadn't heard from his mother again. He sounded sulky. He wanted to know what other countries in the world had the death penalty and which ones didn't.

Luann finally reached them at home after dinner. She said the call would be brief. She had to keep the line open for Hobart. She would have to talk him through the rest of the night. Prison officials would come for him two hours before the execution. She would accompany him to the execution holding cell, Room LL. She would witness the procedure from the adjacent execution viewing room. Now, speaking to Adam, her voice was steady and controlled. She again itemized the miscarriages of justice undertaken by the State of Oklahoma, including those that predated the crime. Hobart had never received the medical and psychological care that he needed and had a right to. The police had compromised their own review of the investigation. The local public defenders hadn't mounted an aggressive defense nor properly questioned the prospective jurors. The jury hadn't been racially balanced. The higher courts hadn't properly reviewed the judgment. There were still questions about the facts of the case, but Hobart Stubbs was being put to death anyway.

Adam said, "It was kind of inevitable."

The silence on the other end of the call was like the quiet of deep space. He and Luann had an exceptionally good connection. The moments prolonged themselves. Adam knew he had misspoken.

"Right," she said.

Adam could have backtracked. He could have said he meant the man's fate was determined the day he was born in that skin and in those circumstances. He could have said that, given that skin, given those circumstances, no one could have done a better job defending Hobart Stubbs than she had. Only the brute force of a dishonest state government had defeated her. But she had been heroic. All this was true. Oddly, though, Adam didn't say a thing.

Only after the call with Luann, and then after some time staring at the wall, did Adam call Valerie, though he hadn't forgotten about her in the course of the afternoon, not during the editorial meeting, not during the urgent phone calls afterward, not during dinner with his anguished son, and not during his call with Luann. The imprint of her lips was still on his.

"Hey, I'm sorry."

This was inadequate. *Sorry*—what a goddamn lame word. Something you said when you accidentally brushed against someone on the Metro. That wasn't what he felt now, even if the verbal expression of what he felt eluded him. Multiform regret coursed through his arteries and his veins and his every last fucking capillary. At the same time he keenly realized that he had screwed up his conversation with Luann.

"No, that's OK," Valerie said lightly.

"You were expecting me."

"Not really."

She *hadn't* been expecting him? The lack of expectation would have meant something. It would have meant that she thought he never intended to come back to resolve what happened in the Chi-Chi's restroom. It would have meant that she always believed his help with her story, his interest in her career, and his friendship had been ungenuine. It would have meant that *she* had never entertained the hope of a romantic relationship with him. That the first kiss had meant nothing to her. But it wasn't true. She *had* been expecting him at four o'clock. Now it was past nine. She had been forced to rethink her expectations. She may have used the five hours to rethink the entire arc of her romantic life.

"I wanted to come over. But then Luann lost her appeals. She took it hard and so did Jason. The execution's happening tomorrow morning. So it was a bit of a family crisis."

"Right. I understand," Valerie said levelly. "Too bad about the case. You said Luann had thrown everything into it."

"Listen, Valerie."

"What?"

"I'm sorry," he repeated. "I can't come over now. But we need to talk. About what happened. What it meant. How about tomorrow? Not early. It has to be after the execution, six a.m. their time, in case Luann needs to call. But how about late morning? I can bring bagels."

"What's the point, Adam?"

"Our friendship. I only want to make sure we get our friendship back to where it was," he said pleadingly. But he recognized that the place to where he wanted to return the friendship contained a possibly unlocked room that might still accommodate the potential for romance. A bed. "C'mon, we can call it brunch."

She made an abrupt, barely audible snort. In that little sound lay a dead, hypersaline ocean of bitterness. "I don't do brunch," she said. "Breakfast delayed is breakfast denied."

Adam said, "I'm sorry you're mad."

"I'm not mad," she said, her voice still even. "I'm relieved. We went too far. My fault, really."

"How was it your fault? I wanted it as much as you did."

She asked crisply, "Wanted *what*, Adam?"

This was a solid question. After the Chi-Chi's restroom, what had he wanted to happen next? Hopefully actually successful lovemaking in her *boudoir*? And then? More lovemaking indefinitely? Would they grow old like that, together? Is that what he thought *Valerie* envisioned?

"I don't know," he confessed. "I'm confused. I was thinking only in the moment. I'm thinking only in the moment now."

Her voice softening, to give the impression that none of this was a big deal, she observed, "I'm having some weird effect on men lately."

"Valerie!" he protested, not wanting to be categorized with other men.

"Maybe I have to change my perfume."

"Wait. You wear perfume?"

There were still so many things he didn't know about her. That he would never know.

She said wearily, "Good night, Adam."

Valerie completed and emailed her two already-assigned pieces without coming into the office. Adam never met her for lunch again. Max made no remark about her not writing for them any longer.

Adam wondered what she would do next. He hadn't expected her to leave Washington, the city where she could best exploit her talents and expertise. She belonged in the capital. In the *Next Deal*'s staff box. She belonged somewhere close. He poked and fingered this little hole in his heart, but her departure was hardly the most consequential change in his life.

Luann had attended the execution, eye to eye with Hobart before the shutters in the death chamber went down. The shutters went down when the drugs were administered, a weird legal nicety meant to respect the man's privacy. They went back up when the drugs started to take effect. Hobart found her eyes again, but she would never speak of what this meant to her. Afterward she remained in Oklahoma to attend the funeral that she had arranged for him. Her colleagues had to talk her down when she threatened to bury Hobart in the same cemetery as his victims, one last stick in the eye of the family that had declined to meet her when she was asking for clemency. She returned five days later without any glow at all. Instead, as she entered the house, she showed a new determination, as fierce as it ever was.

She announced that she was leaving her job with the ACLU. Adam was stunned and disappointed. She was so good at it, how could she leave? She shrugged. She said she wasn't saving anybody. Her ineffective lawyerly efforts to defend the wrongly condemned only validated the system. The system was profoundly wicked.

She would be shortly hired as a litigator at one of the capital's top corporate firms, for a salary so stupendous that he guffawed when she told him what it was. They were breaking up, but he guffawed anyway. She would go on to pay for Jason's college and theological seminary without blinking an eye. Even after she made partner, she continued to live modestly, even frugally, and alone, investing her money and time in after-school programs and pre-crime intervention. She became deeply involved in a mentorship program for young high school women, getting them through their classes and their sometimes-difficult family situations, and into a state of mind where, like Jason, they could seriously expect to go to college.

"But if you get knocked up," she warned them, "you're dead to me."

These days Luann was a leading member of more than one public interest board and a significant figure in the social justice community. Adam saw her name in the paper. The states kept putting people to death, of course, but lives were saved every year.

THE DAY WAS STILL YOUNG. So, evidently, was the news cycle. Now other women journalists were coming forward to complain about Max, most of them women Adam knew either personally or from their bylines. A few had been interns at the magazine and one of them, at the time, had just graduated from *high school*. Yikes. Most of these accusations belonged to the category of misjudged amatory maneuvers. Not all the women had worked at the *Next Deal*, but enough had worked there to make plain a baleful pattern. What one learned from it was that the charming, accomplished, hyperliterate Max Lieberthol was dismally awkward with women and had tried to use his position to sleep with them.

Other offenses were more tangible: a hand on a jeaned butt, the same hand brushed against another woman's breast, an unwanted hug, an unwanted back rub. There were three—count 'em, three—lunges at three surprised faces. One woman testified that, after accompanying her back from the hotel bar at the 2004 Democratic National Convention in Boston, Max had forced himself into her room. To get him out, she had to threaten to call 911. This was the night of the Obama speech.

The woman was using an anonymous Twitter handle, but Adam knew who she was: a famous drinker and voting demographics whiz. She was the one who had flagged a Dem vulnerability that year among soccer moms in Bucks County, Pennsylvania. Adam had been in Boston, too, for an article about John Kerry, and he had seen her and Max palling around. He could believe the story.

Only one of the women who had been physically harassed identified herself. The other incidents were reported either anonymously or by witnesses who withheld the name of the victim or by second- and thirdhand sources. The greater the offense, the further distance there was from the accusation. Yet the character of the predator was emerging credibly, recognizably. A minor-league predator, perhaps, but no one was making those distinctions right now.

Adam's confirmation of Valerie's charge was of course the clincher, the substantiation of every anecdote and hearsay and rumor and guess. Adam was still getting shit for not confirming it at the time. If Adam had, if Adam had come forward then, Max's depredations might not have been visited upon the other women, including the "high school girl." Adam murmured to the screen that she had been about to start college. Dartmouth. Then the outrage ballooned well

beyond Max, Adam, and the *Next Deal* to encompass
the entire question, or entrenched phenomenon, of
sexual harassment by the Washington media elite. A
few other cases had already been reported. More epi-
sodes were apparently waiting only for their victims to
announce themselves.

Valerie's article was really shaking some trees. Forget
Max. How was *Adam* going to hold on?

Max had asked him if he had ever been romantically
involved with a woman in which there hadn't been some
inequality in status or power.

No, probably not.

Adam had snagged his first girlfriend when he was
in the twelfth grade. She was in tenth and obviously
impressed with herself for what she thought was her elevation into adult society. He had a *driver's license*. They
drove the suburban roads of Virginia and Maryland
for hours at a time, and once to West Virginia, talking
about serious things like nineteenth-century novels,
progressive jazz, and who they thought they were.
They French-kissed at stoplights. He copped a feel.
She placed her hand on his lap. And there had been
three occasions, once on a tarp-covered couch being
stored in her parents' basement—even though her
mother was upstairs clamorously making dinner—and
once in the back seat of his parents' fuel-efficient but
otherwise infelicitous Le Car, and once on a blanket

at a late-night picnic in Rock Creek Park, that technically, if not elegantly, could be defined as intercourse.
Now, *she* had been a high school girl.

Even with Luann something unequal had been
going on. She came to the Ivy League from an almost
comically backward region of Georgia, tobacco farm-
land and whatnot. Adam posed as the suave northerner,
proud to be the first Jewish person she had ever met.
He could play that up, dropping completely unfamiliar
Anglo-Yiddishisms left and right: *meshugga*, *shmegegge*,
and, post facto, *shtup*. He was the Other, with all the
exotic qualities that implied, and she could employ his
Otherness to demonstrate to her parents how far she had
gone, how far she had gone *from them*. He and Luann
used to call the place Dogpatch, and not only between
themselves.

And then he had to ask himself how many times
had alcohol *not* been involved in anything romantic?
The romance wasn't governed only by the inebriation.
The agreement to drink was also a signal of interest.
But it was also the inebriation. He and Luann had
always drunk. He had probably been the one to sug-
gest the margaritas at Chi-Chi's. He may have found
significance in Valerie's ready agreement. He couldn't
blame Max for thinking he had gotten the demog-
rapher drunk enough in Boston. Max had probably
been drunk enough himself to think he had gotten her
drunk enough.

Among its other virtues, alcohol could persuade you and the other person that what you were about to do meant less than it did.

A pass was a risky maneuver. An incomplete pass, the one the presumed receiver declined to catch, the one the presumed receiver free in the end zone apparently waving their arms may have never seen coming, could destroy a friendship. And now you were discovering that it could also destroy reputations, careers, and legacies.

Meanwhile, people continued to fall in love, often in less-than-pristine circumstances. At least half the couples he knew had met professionally, almost never in precisely the same professional positions. Other couples he knew had first been acquaintances or casual friends. These relationships had taken time to become romantic. Some of the complications may have been awkward or worse than awkward: embarrassing, demeaning, or offensive. These complications may have generated hairline cracks in what now appeared to be solid, long-lasting relationships. The chance of untoward complications was taken at the start of every romance.

Adam was thinking now that a plausible letter could be written in defense of Max. But Adam wasn't going to write it. Let one of the other luminaries write it, one of the luminaries whose personal histories weren't knotted with morally dubious entanglements.

The Chi-Chi's was now a Panera, which he passed every time he went to his urologist. Not so often, but still. The single-occupancy public restroom presumably continued to locate itself off the lobby on the way to the elevators. Its fixtures were probably the same. Twenty years later, forensics might even find something on the slate.

Adam should have closed his Twitter account to direct messages long ago, but he lived in hope that someone real would slide in with a fresh insight on a story he was covering or with a credible lead on another story that could be pursued. That hardly ever happened. Mostly he got abuse from trolls. Today his DMs were going crazy, predictably. Most of the texts were labeling him as some variety of shithead. Nothing new there. He scrolled through quickly.

Wait a minute.

I didn't want you to get involved.

The message was from @viovine. Adam checked his feed to confirm the address. Yes, she was @viovine. This was his first communication from Valerie Iovine in twenty years, since the phone call late on the night when Hobart Stubbs's appeals ran out, dating from seven years before the world's first Twitter message had been conceived. No salutation, no nothing. He wrote back at once.

It was unavoidable. I don't mind.

Adam watched the screen. A minute went by, and then two. Would that constitute the whole exchange?

The sum of the two former friends' twenty-first-century correspondence? Patience, he counseled himself. Social media's immediacy and ego-gratification devices worked against patience. Everything worked against patience. The next minute passed too. That seemed to be it, all she had to say. He continued to stare at the screen. He checked his mail. Nothing from MSNBC either. Damn. Back to Twitter. Finally, her handle popped up again.

I mind.

People were challenging you. I thought I was helping.

More silence. It was like communicating with another world located a certain number of light-minutes away. He had too much time to think while the DMs sluggishly made their way across the interplanetary medium. He tried to picture Valerie at the other end of the connection, as she was now, not as she was twenty years ago. Now she was standing by herself on a rusty, sandy planet swept by hundred-mile-an-hour winds. He recalled his confusion the moment he gave in to Aurelie Dumesnil's questioning. He had known Valerie didn't want him to come forward.

Adam.

What.

What happened was with Max. That's my focus.

I know.

What happened with you isn't part of the story.

Adam had hoped they could get through this without reference to what had happened with him. At least it was a general reference. He was still surprised to find Valerie on the screen. That it took a major social movement like #MeToo for them to be in contact again.

Right. I told them only about Max.

I'm under a microscope, she DM'd with a detectable note of complaint. Adam wasn't going to tell her that she only felt like she was under a microscope, that the feeling was a feature, not a bug, of social media. *I'm being judged for everything I've ever written, everything I've done, everything that's happened to me. I don't want our thing to be part of it.*

It won't be, he assured her.

People will look at what happened and say I was foolish and irresponsible.

Was she the one who had been irresponsible? He hadn't thought of it that way. He had, as usual, been thinking only of himself, his desires, his actions. Adam had feared that she would bring up their relationship, but he smiled now at the new euphemism. "Our thing." He felt renewed warmth at the thought of Valerie Iovine, of the bright, affectionate woman at twenty-six, this acknowledgment that what happened was something shared, and that she was also sharing responsibility for it. "Our thing." Yes, it had been just one of those things, a trip to the moon on gossamer wings.

Adam felt moved to respond: *I was irresponsible too. I cared for you. I wasn't thinking straight.*

As if what happened with you was the same as with Max.

No, of course it wasn't.

Adam had always known that no valid comparison could be made between their romance-inflected friendship and Max's sexual harassment. He and Valerie had not only shared a mutual affection, they had demonstrated it to each other. He had come to reconsider their encounter and reproach himself only because of #MeToo. He had been overly alarmed, once she went public, only because of the proximity of her incident with Max.

Adam recognized his tendency to overthink things. His judiciousness might have served as an advantage when it came to the public policy issues he was writing about, but he could also exhaust himself working through every aspect of his personal imbroglios. He had dwelled a little too intensely on the situation with Valerie. He scrolled up through the conversation and observed the residual affection that she evidently held for him. Of course she did. He held affection for her too. He had regretted for two decades the loss of their friendship. He had seen it as a personal failure. He reminded himself now that they had both been adults at the time.

She DM'd, *It was worse.*

He recoiled hard against the back of his chair. Then he brought his face close to the screen and the blazing line of type, as if it required further study. Now he was the one who didn't immediately respond. He realized, sickeningly, that he hadn't been overthinking things enough.

He wrote back, lamely, *What do you mean?*

This was unconsidered. This was stupid. Adam wished Twitter had a function that allowed you to withdraw direct messages. What she meant was the last thing he wanted to DM about.

She may not have wanted to DM about it either. It was a long while before she replied, *I'm talking about the restroom.*

I know.

He wished he and Valerie could have another conversation right now on another subject, IRL, F2F, just to catch up. Despite the deep Google search, despite his attempt at constructing from it a narrative of her life since 1999, he really knew nothing about her. Was she really still single? She knew nothing about him. At the very least, he would have told her that Jason had become a rabbi.

She wrote, *What you did.*

We did, he corrected her. *I thought it was something we did together. I thought it was consensual.*

Another pause. It was probably unwise to correct her. No, definitely unwise.

He added an amendment: *Well, kind of. Semiconsensual.*

A full two minutes passed before she responded.

Semi.

The four letters stared back at him with contempt.

I thought there was at least some mutual desire.

How could you think that.

We were close.

Not in that way.

All that time in your bedroom.

We were working together. It just happened to be my bedroom.

He recalled the bedroom. The bed. Her weight on the bed, next to his, as if it were yesterday.

She added, *You were married, Adam. I wouldn't think of getting involved.*

Those things happen.

There were no signals.

He reminded her, *The kiss outside the restaurant.*

You kissed me!

I thought YOU kissed ME.

No.

He insisted, *You kissed me back.*

No I didn't. You forced me into the restroom.

You allowed me to.

I didn't!!!! You're bigger, stronger than me!!!!

Adam was five feet, eight inches tall and these days he weighed about 175 pounds, maybe fifteen more than he had then. Hardly a bruiser, and she was hardly petite, but it was true, she had certainly weighed less than he did.

The exclamation marks were another cause for alarm. Old pressmen used to call them bangers.

And he had indeed applied force. He again revisited the effort. He pressed against the top of his desk, trying to repeat it, to measure it, wondering how many joules qualified as physical coercion. She had expended some effort in return.

He wrote, *I thought there was willingness on your part.*

She waited awhile before she responded. Maybe he should have said "believed," to have made his assertion stronger. But he hadn't wanted to provoke her further.

I said No.

This was absolutely correct. She had been clear and direct. She had repeated her refusal. He could hear her voice now as it was then in the lobby, close to his ear, moistening the inner flap.

And these days "active affirmation" was the rule for both partners engaged in sexual activity. They were each required to say or in some way communicate yes. But had Adam *ever* received active affirmation at the beginning of a sexual encounter? And then at every stage of the encounter? "May I kiss you?" "Yes you may." "May I touch your breasts?" "Yes you may." Well, yes, once, back in college, freshman year, but that had come at the conclusion of a strenuous flirtation, and it was kind of a joke, and he already had his arms around the woman, and, again, they were both drunk. Adam couldn't think of a single romantic situation in which he, as a man, hadn't waged some kind of campaign to prove his interest and in which the woman (and there had really been only a handful) hadn't felt obliged to put up a show of resistance. And did *no* always mean no? No. In his experience, no could be an invitation to try harder. Unless she meant no. You didn't need to be a genius to figure out when no really meant no, but then, apparently, evidently, spectacularly, in these situations men were often much less than geniuses.

He felt ungentlemanly defending himself: *But you were acting otherwise.*

Adam, I admit I was confused. She must have scrolled up through their DM exchange too. *I should have never got myself into that position with you, that close. I liked you, you were caring at a time when I needed help. That's why I didn't want to involve you now. But I never gave you any kind of permission.*

Valerie, I swear you kissed me back. And I thought you were responsive. He reached back for the memory of a soughing, a murmur, a quickening of respiration. *There were sounds of satisfaction.*

A physiological response. That doesn't mean anything. I still said NO.

This was a well-established legal and moral principle: involuntary physical reactions didn't qualify as agreement or even pleasure. He was a jerk for bringing it up. But still he recalled the most intimate details of their encounter. What it felt like. He thought that should count for something.

He DM'd, *You opened the buttons on your slacks.*

You were going to tear them!!!!! You were like a wild man. I said no. I resisted. You put me under pressure.

I was trying to show my desire.

Another pause in her responses. Was she contemplating his desire? Was she recalling her own? Did she remember that, if it weren't for the editorial meeting, they were going to return to her apartment?

She DM'd, *Right, you did a number on the floor of the restroom.*

She remembered that too. Of course she did—she remembered everything. They both did. Adam scrolled back through the exchange, watching it as it went bad, sliding from top to bottom on the screen, which was like all the other screens upon which we conducted our lives, separating us from one another, shadowing us behind an alkali-aluminosilicate veil of obscurity. He wished that she had at least sent a smiley face.

He didn't know how to reply. Several retorts came to mind, but he realized he wasn't in the mood to make them. He wondered if he was too hurt.

She wrote, *I thought you were my friend. But you just wanted to fuck me.*

He shot back, furious, *Not mutually exclusive.*

Would you say that to a gay friend who made a pass at you? Who forced you into a restroom to have sex with you?

Adam had one close gay friend. The idea was disgusting.

But you're not gay!

So you think that makes me a willing sexual partner for any man?

I wasn't any man.

In that restroom you were.

She might as well have slapped him full in the face. That was what this felt like. His face stung and continued to burn. He hadn't thought of her as any woman.

He could write back only, *Yeah, right.*

She didn't reply.

NO LETTER WAS PRODUCED by any of the journalistic and intellectual A-listers that Max had mentioned. No one was coming to Max's defense, except for Alan Dershowitz.

Max, however, issued his own statement, which was sent to the major news organizations, the only ones he cared about. The few terse lines quickly found their way onto Twitter, conveyed predominantly by retweets of derision.

"I am sadly aware of charges that have been leveled against me related to a distant episode. They are untrue. Recollections can differ. Objective fact cannot. A full, accurate explanation of the incident under fraudulent discussion will appear in the next issue of the *Next Deal*, available at newsstands June 21."

At newsstands? Max really *was* a dinosaur.

The magazine would never run Max's defense. Early that afternoon, while Adam was still waiting for one last DM from Valerie, his anxiety deepening, a dozen very prominent women journalists and critics issued a declaration that they wouldn't write for the *Next Deal* as long as Max remained editor. Most of them had never written for the *Next Deal* and would have been unlikely to. The magazine paid too poorly. Further refusals from other writers and people who hoped to be writers followed on Twitter.

This worked. A one-sentence announcement from the associate publisher shortly declared that Max had resigned. The associate publisher's name was unfamiliar to anyone in Washington. She had never had anything to do with the magazine's editorial matters; the job was strictly administrative. She reported directly to the owners in Jamaica. She may have been in Jamaica herself.

Max made no further statement, which was almost as newsworthy as the news of his departure.

Despite the quick firing, criticism of the *Next Deal* continued to build. The affair occasioned the revoicing of venerable complaints about the magazine. Max's personal failings seemed to validate everything wrong about his politics and even everything wrong with political journalism, especially as it was performed by men.

The *Times* called.

"Hey Aurelie," Adam said, as if she were an old friend, as if every deflector shield wasn't raised, as if he didn't know his every word was on the record.

"You know Max is gone, right?"

"I saw," he said, sounding just a touch sad. That was how he had to play it.

"Your confirmation of Valerie's story made his situation untenable," she said, commending herself for reporting it first. "That's what did it."

"I guess."

"This must hurt. You had such a long association with Max."

Adam demurred, repeating that he had written for the *Next Deal* only off and on. He was still determined to give her as little as possible. He kept his regrets anodyne, saying Max had made valuable contributions to the political conversation over the years. It was unfortunate that his tenure at the *Next Deal* was ending this way, but the focus should be on changing the Washington media culture going forward. He liked saying, this afternoon, the words "going forward."

But after getting off the phone Adam couldn't help wondering what Max would do now. He was just seventy, still in good health, still going strong. He had written cogently in the last issue about the threat posed by antiabortion legislation making its way through several state legislatures in wait for an anti-*Roe* Supreme Court majority. He wouldn't get another editorial job, of course. Would he freelance? Write political essays? No, not now at least. He was suspect and so were his political opinions. Perhaps he could write a book. But who would publish it? Publishers were especially skittish these days, and not only about public opinion. Their own editors and employees, even $35K-a-year editorial assistants tripling up in Crown Heights, were capable of revolt.

Adam was fortunately dropped to the bottom of the new article by the time it was posted. The story was moving quickly, as almost every story did these days. Who even remembered Trump's threat of an anti-immigration tariff against Mexico two weeks ago? By the article's fourth paragraph, the subject had mostly shifted to the question of Max's likely successor, though no candidates were named.

You'd have to think the next editor would be a woman. As institutions across society reckoned with their histories of sexual harassment, the appointment of women to leadership positions had become almost imperative. They were seen as the most effective agents for changing an enterprise's office culture and, though no one ever said this outright, their elevation may have been considered some kind of redress or payback. Adam immediately thought of Charlotte Skinner. She would be a name editor with hands-on journalistic experience, a former *Next Deal* stalwart, admired enough to restore prestige to the battered publication. He had seen her last month at the State Department going head-to-head with their spokesperson on behalf of the *Daily Beast*. She still had great legs. She would be an obvious choice—unless they wanted someone younger, to reverse the precipitous aging of the magazine's readership. These days the back cover usually carried an ad for a cruise line. The magazine could also use someone who cared about the website, which Max had seen as an afterthought, and social media, which Max had dismissed as inconsequential, ha ha.

The succession would give the city's media types something to chew on for the next several days. With Max gone, Valerie's charges against him would swiftly become old news. If Adam could stay off Twitter, his role in the affair would, hopefully, go down the memory hole. When it came to the news these days, it was like everyone had Alzheimer's, and there were more than enough #MeToo cases coming down the pike. Not that Adam was going to forget anything that happened between him and Valerie, no matter how much protein plaque was accumulated by his neural tissue, any more than Valerie would. She was still out there, seething.

Adam tried to go back to his own article. What was it about? He had forgotten the story he was working on as completely as he had when he was sitting across Valerie's desk in her bedroom. He couldn't even determine the subject from looking at the file name. The deadline was approaching fast.

He read their DM thread again, twice, in sorrow. He had underestimated Valerie's anger from the beginning, especially the self-anger lurking in her regret for having been fond of him. That anger went back twenty years. It had matured. #MeToo had put it in a social and political context. #MeToo had given it meaning. And then there was his fucking *semiconsensual*.

He realized that Valerie would be obliged now to respond to Max's departure from the magazine.

She took a long hour. The whole of Twitter waited, or rather it was the impatient, infinitesimal, political feminist news media industry subset of Twitter that felt like the whole to the users inside it. When she finally issued a statement, the tweet was hardly less bland than Adam's comments to the *Times*. Valerie wrote that this episode involved only a single woman journalist, a single male editor, and a single rectification.

More TK, she added.

She ended with *#MeToo*.

Her reticence was in keeping with her latter-day character. But the *TK*, journalistic shorthand for "to come," was usually a note to oneself or an editor about a missing detail or comment. It was unnerving here. Yes, there was more to come in order to understand the grip that sexism exerted upon the windpipe of the nation's political journalism. Stories were underplayed. Stories were missed. People were hurt. But Adam intuited that more specific information might be contained within Valerie's *TK*. Boy, was she angry.

The ramifications of Max's exit continued to echo through the media. Dozens of personal messages came in to Adam, mostly from writer friends commenting on the firing and what it meant for the future of progressive journalism—some think pieces were gestating. Most of the texts expressed condolences that he had gotten mixed up in the affair. A few offered wrong-key congratulations for sending Max into an overdue retirement.

There was nothing further from Valerie's Twitter account, even while her latest tweet was retweeted well into the thousands. More than one person found something deliberately ambiguous about it. As well as something promising.

Oh wait. Here's a tweet. Adam has been scrolling and refreshing. This is at the top of his feed and it already has thirty likes. A strange tweet, hashtagged *#Lieberlover*, *#UnsubscribeNDeal*, and, most ominously, *#falsefriend*. The tweet is not from @viovine.

TK: Consent is a legal term, not a moral value. Consent is morally absent in circumstances of inequality. And falseness.

This was followed moments later by a self-reply.

Male media's morally absent. A lifeless ocean, a toxic river. Harassment flows well beyond the editor's office. It seeps through ostensible collegiality, friendship. It gushes through the office spaces, the lunch places. Not every campaign for sexual conquest is soaked in glory.

This was followed moments later by a second self-reply, a seven-character tweet that shot through the ether like a thunderbolt, unerringly aimed, it seemed, at the mortal center of Adam's beating heart.

The tweet read simply, *@azweig*.

Twitter discourse was strange, its rules and conventions still evolving, and some people were just not good at it. Jokes fell flat. Sarcastic remarks and parodies arrived without being signified as such. Misspellings and dropped words generated misunderstanding and, not even to mention covfefe, hilarity. People didn't use hashtags correctly. Not everything made sense. Some users might now wonder why the third tweet tagged the political writer who confirmed Valerie Iovine's charges against Max Lieberthol. What did it mean? They would continue to wonder.

The tweets were credited to an account, @wtrapped, that appeared to have been opened only today, but it already had a few followers. It would gain more. There was no bio note. Adam allowed himself to speculate that it was a troll. Possibly. Possibly even Russian, from Glavset, the GRU-connected Saint Petersburg troll farm, from some operative whose specialty was fucking with American liberal legacy media. But it wasn't the Russians. It was someone who knew something, someone like a friend of Valerie's, someone in whom she had once confided. No, it wasn't a friend. Adam was forced to accept that @wtrapped was Valerie herself, using a burner account.

She was pissed off, for sure. She was pissed off *at him.*

He wasn't going to get any work done today. He'd have to convince the *Guardian* that the health insurance story could wait another week. Next week suddenly seemed like a very distant part of his life. Fuck. Had they seen this at MSNBC? Of course they had.

The posts were being retweeted, accompanied by diverse exegeses. Many retweeters elaborated on the spurious nature of sexual consent, which was often granted under duress or cognitive impairment, or subject to chicanery or illusion. By male hook or by male crook. Many commentators understood that the post had to do with what happened at the *Next Deal*. Something more than what had happened inside Max's office. Something worse, and also that it had to do with Adam.

"Not every campaign for sexual conquest is soaked in glory."

Yeah, no kidding. He didn't care for the liquid spillage metaphors.

He looked again at the name of the account, @wtrapped. It must mean something. You couldn't come up with a totally unrevealingly named burner account, any more than you could pull out of your head an untraceable password. Even the laying on of fingers upon random keys revealed your predilections and secrets. *Trapped?*

All right, he thought he understood that. It probably reflected her feeling of the moment, locked inside the cage of the patriarchy. Or locked inside the cage of social media attention. It was an odd word choice, but maybe the first that came to mind.

But *w*? What was that about?

It might have been no more than a typo when she hurriedly set up the account. But Adam stared at it, thinking that it must be an abbreviation for something else. Woman? Woman Trapped? Womb? War? World? Wolf?

Wolf.

Got it. Wolf Trap was the concert venue in Fairfax County. Valerie's dashed plans to attend the Del McCoury concert there had signified the end of her romantic relationship with Josef twenty years ago. This spoke of a long personal history that didn't involve either Adam or Max, of something that related to other disappointments, but looked back to the spring of 1999 anyway, a season of personal confusion and distress. In creating this fake identity, Valerie was returning to a time of several painful encounters. Adam was one of them. The handle was a very private memorial to the ill-used young woman she had once been. She hadn't intended for anyone to understand. For Adam to have figured it out was like another violation.

Or . . . *shit.* Wolf *Trapped.* What was trapped was the wolf. Him. *Him?* This may have been more than her subconscious at work.

Valerie wanted to expose Adam as a false friend and something worse than a false friend—how did *rapist* sound?—without directly exposing herself to challenge. There was no direct link from @viovine to @wtrapped. Clumsy, Adam thought, but not ineffective. People would get it.

He was being messaged left and right now, mostly along the lines of *Hey, what went on between you and Valerie Iovine anyway?* So far, at least, @wtrapped's tweets remained too vague to be picked up by the news sites. But the amplitude of comments would overwhelm the accusation's ambiguity soon enough, and some reporter would have to run with it. The tweets, texts, and DMs kept arriving.

But one phone text came in that was off topic.

Lucked out this year with Bellinger, Shane Bieber, and Pete Alonso! How about you? Hey call me.

Bellinger was a Dodger, Bieber was an Indian, and Alonso was a rookie Met, all of them having good seasons. The texter, however, was Damon Brosseau, the quant dude he interviewed years ago for the high-frequency trading story, one of the guys who had bought the *Next Deal*.

Adam stared at the text for a while, even while new messages were arriving, including one, of course, from Aurelie Dumesnil. He didn't want to talk to her. That seemed to leave him no option but to call Damon Brosseau.

"Yo, I just landed. I can stay on only a minute."

"That's fine," Adam said. "We can talk another time, if it can wait . . ."

"Did you know, I'm the *Next Deal*'s co-owner? I just flew in. Silas is at some weed legalization convention. So I'm supposed to straighten out this Max thing."

Adam had guessed the call was about Max, though he was impressed that Damon had Bieber and Alonso. He wondered if the quant had cracked the fantasy base-ball code.

"Yeah, it's too bad about what happened," Adam said neutrally.

"I saw your name in the paper!" Damon exclaimed. "*The New York* fucking *Times*! Congratulations."

"Right," Adam said, stifling the urge to tell him that this was the eleventh time his name had been in the paper, in one of its news stories, not counting his bylines in the *Book Review*, the *Magazine*, and the opinion section. And there would be a twelfth once the *Times* reported that social media was speculating about his deeper involvement with Valerie. But he was pleased Damon had mentioned it anyway. "Thank you," he said.

Damon confessed, "I really don't know Washington at all. I mean, I want to see the Washington Monument and the Air and Space Museum, but I have to figure out who's going to run the magazine. That's why I'm here. I saw you in the paper and thought maybe you can give me some names of who to talk to? You know people, right?"

"Yes, of course. I've already been thinking about it. I might have some ideas for you."

"*Fan*tastic!" Damon said. "Can you meet me for a drink a little later, once I get settled?"

"Sure," Adam said quickly, as if getting away from his home office would get him away from Twitter. As if it would get him away from the *Times* reporter. As if it would get him away from his personal history with Valerie Iovine. "I can do that."

"I'm staying at the Trump Hotel. How about the bar at four?"

Damon laughed at Adam's stunned silence. He would have laughed even harder if he had seen Adam's face.

Still chuckling, Damon said, "Don't worry, I hate the guy. Mr. Comb-Over. But I heard so much about the hotel, I wanted to see it. You don't mind, do you?"

For a story, Adam had once gone inside the core of a decommissioned nuclear reactor—the story was about how its decommissioning had been botched. Another time, in Afghanistan, he had flown into a forward operating base being shelled by the Taliban. He had spent a night doing the rounds with the staff at Rikers. He supposed he could enter the Trump International Hotel. But, really, were people still talking about his hair?

"That's OK," he said. "Four o'clock."

Adam heard on the other end of the line a flight attendant thank Mr. Brosseau for flying with them, a little extra honey in her voice. He must have been traveling first class.

"Got to get off," Damon said. "But tell me, who do you have?"

"Well, Charlotte Skinner, for one. No one knows this town better than she does."

"No, you can tell me later. I mean on your team this year."

"I'm not playing," Adam said ruefully. "The primaries are coming up—I have to focus on that."

"Boy, you reporters never stop. It's like politics is your fantasy baseball."

After the call ended, the remark lingered in Adam's ears. He was puzzled by the sarcastic equivalency. First, did Damon not realize that Adam did this for a living? Or was Damon so rich that he could no longer distinguish between work and a pastime? But, more worryingly, did Damon not recognize that the fate of American democracy rested on the next election? That issues vital to the nation's future—the rule of law, the climate emergency, access to health care—would have to be decided within the next seventeen short months? It occurred to Adam that the co-owner of one of the nation's great political magazines thought politics was less interesting than fantasy baseball. A *lot* of people evidently thought that politics was less interesting than a lot of things.

ADAM FINALLY PICKED UP in the Uber.

"Those are some curious tweets going around," Aurelie Dumesnil said casually, now as if he were the old friend. As if he hadn't managed not to answer her calls for the past hour.

"I guess."

"I haven't been able to reach Valerie," Aurelie confided. "She's just not answering her phone or replying to texts."

She sounded offended. People at the *Times* got like that the first fifteen minutes they worked there.

"I don't think she cares for publicity," Adam said. "I mean, coming forward about Max had to be difficult."

"Sure, but what about *these* tweets? And why did she @ you?"

"We don't know they're from her."

"No, we don't," she conceded gullibly. "But it's certainly someone with an intimate knowledge of what was happening at the *Next Deal*."

"Or not. It could be a troll. Making trouble."

"Right. But Adam, I still have to ask you about the tweets."

"I understand. I've already conceded that I should have reported Max's behavior. I let Valerie down. I still deeply regret this."

"But these tweets are something new. 'Harassment flows well beyond the editor's office.' What does that mean? It looks like she's claiming something further untoward occurred. People are guessing that it involves you."

"If it's her."

"Or it's somebody who knows something."

"If they do."

"All right then," Aurelie said, realizing he was trying to elude her polite, indirect questioning. "Adam, are you denying anything improper occurred?"

"Aurelie, we don't know who's making the charge or what the charge is. But nothing improper happened."

"Nothing of a sexual nature?"

He made a sound that suggested he was trying not to laugh at the question's absurdity. Then he said gravely, "There was nothing like that, Aurelie."

They chased around the issue for a few more minutes, but she couldn't nail him down on anything so
slippery. She knew he was being evasive. Adam was
sadly confident that she would eventually get the story,
or at least some story. He warmly wished her good luck
on the article and then, once they ended the call, wondered whether she might be hit by a bus within the next
hour or at least get hired at Columbia. He would have
been sweating heavily if the Uber wasn't overchilled. He
sneezed instead.

As the car approached the former Old Post Office
building on Pennsylvania Avenue, the goddamn Trump
Hotel, he tried to distract himself. He observed the
tourists milling near the souvenir stands and the food
trucks. These few blocks had become a small tourist
locus. He wished he could still think of the nineteenth-
century building as the Old Post Office. It had in fact
stopped being a post office around the time of the First
World War, but the landmark with its distinctive clock
tower had been preserved as a federal office building.
Now it had been ruined, like so much else of the
capital's mental geography, virtually erasing the old
associations. Trump had reneged on his commitments
to preserve the structure's historic features. Once he
was elected, he mandated that his inaugural parties
and balls be held there. He then vastly overcharged the
ostensibly nonprofit Republican inaugural committee.
Lobbyists and visiting foreign leaders were now obliged

to book rooms, some of them paying $10,000 a night. Fuck the Emoluments Clause. Even Secret Service agents protecting him and his family were overcharged for using the hotel.

Adam tried to focus on his meeting with Damon Brosseau. Damon sounded like a well-meaning guy. If the *Next Deal* could put the Max situation behind itself and get back on track, that would be good for everybody, and especially for the Democrats as they headed into the next challenging election against an inexplicably popular incumbent.

Charlotte Skinner seemed to be the smartest and safest choice as Max's replacement. She had a sophisticated news sense and an ear for language. She understood the *Next Deal*'s production cycle. She would know how to calm down the printers when the pages were late, probably with a combination of talk sweet and bawdy. He himself got along better with her than he ever did with Max. If she were named, Adam would probably write for the magazine more often, provided he survived the next hour. So would several other writers whom Max had intermittently alienated.

And yet . . . although Skinner would restore the magazine's reputation, she wouldn't necessarily expand its political impact. A white woman editor could simply not be as much of a game changer as a woman who was, say, *Black*. Perhaps that was what the moment called for: a Black woman editor who would shake the liberal

Washington media establishment out of its stupefied
Trump-induced focus on the moment-by-moment gro-
tesqueries. None of the other political magazines were
led by a Black woman. The appointment would be page
one news, at least on a slow news day, if there ever was
one again.

Not many obvious candidates presented themselves.
Few Black women journalists had been associated
with the *Next Deal*. Relatively few were prominent
among the capital's magazine writers. Adam knew that
it was because of the male, disproportionately white,
Ivy League power structure of the Washington media
establishment that there weren't many Black women
journalists who would be obvious candidates. That was
precisely why more Black women editors were needed,
to bring other Black women into the field, to expand
coverage of racial and gender issues, especially where
those issues intersected.

Rolaika Franco was good. He knew her. She had
reported a couple of opioid stories for the magazine
before being hired away by the *Times*, where she was
doing criminal justice. She was already on an editor
track over there, so she was unlikely to leave. Also, she
had two children under five. He winced. No way was
she going to run a magazine with small kids at home.

Adam wondered about Kristina Newhouse, who
had written a fine book about the unsteady progress
of Black emancipation in the Northern states before

the Civil War. She taught at Brown. Although she had never worked as a reporter, she had become a leading public intellectual, frequently commenting on national issues for the *Post*'s opinions section. Her writing was fresh and forceful. She was also gay, militantly so, which would give the magazine some LGBTQ+ cred.

The harsher the criticism of the magazine, the smarter it would be to hire a gay Black woman. It was too bad she wasn't also disabled. They'd have to give her a shitload of money to extract her from academia's sylvan groves, but he sensed that she had a taste for the hurly-burly of political journalism. The position would catapult her into even higher prominence. He wondered what kind of line editor she would be.

Adam knew what he was doing. He was aware that his thinking was based on the candidates' social identities, not on their merits as individuals. This was something that would have appalled him as a young liberal humanist. Favoring someone for the group they supposedly belonged to was offensive for the same reasons that bigotry was: it devalued the individual person. It operated under the assumption that their group affiliation imbued them with certain capabilities and virtues (or faults). In considering Skinner and Kristina Newhouse, he was valuing their group affiliations as more important than their professional abilities.

Nevertheless, persistent inequalities already sorted people according to social identity. If you were going to reverse that, you needed to give some kind of preference to members of certain groups, like Black people and women This could have a tangibly positive effect, especially for the magazine. It was inescapable that by the simple virtue of being a Black woman, so nearly by definition a Washington media outsider, Kristina Newhouse was likely to take the *Next Deal* in a new direction. She was more likely to widen its coverage. She might be more likely to find, hire, and nurture young journalists from marginalized groups who would see stories that more experienced reporters would miss or frame differently.

Adam also recognized that Kristina Newhouse was unlikely to want *him* to write for the magazine, precisely because of his social identity, because he was white, male, straight, and at the doorstep of late middle age. And now, he saw, looking at what was coming up on his phone as he tipped the driver, Twitter was emphasizing the cryptic connection between @viovine, *TK*, and @wtrapped's three tweets, especially the last one. No, that wasn't going to help at all.

Adam stood for a few minutes on the carnival-frenzied sidewalk in front of the hotel plaza. The tweets from @wtrapped had been subjected to every kind of analysis: linguistic, feminist, structuralist, Baudrillardian, Freudian, and post-Freudian. The conclusion was that something sexual had transpired between him and Valerie Iovine at a time when he was a staff writer with editorial responsibilities and she was a freelancer. Twitter demanded confirmation. Twitter demanded elaboration. Twitter was going much further than the *Times* could right now. A few tweeters noted that Adam was, like Max, Jewish, or, more pungently, a *Jew*. They couldn't all be trolls, could they?

BEFORE THIS AFTERNOON, Adam never had a reason to come to the Trump International Hotel, no interview, no press conference, no social occasion. Unlike Damon Brosseau, he had maintained a steadfast lack of curiosity about what Trump had done to the building. Now he felt dirty just passing through the triple-arched entrance beneath the president's gold-lettered name, all capped, and allowing the doorman to spin the heavy revolving door for him.

Once inside he stopped short, startled in spite of himself. The interior was tremendous, much bigger than the office building had ever seemed, its atrium soaring. What had once been mail-sorting facilities had been turned into a vast lobby beneath arched pillars and suspended steel walkways, all of it bathed in a golden late spring radiance pouring down from the skylights. The sofas were upholstered in a deep blue velvet and cream-colored carpets were laid on the dark marble floors. Gold leafing. Wood paneling. Crystal chandeliers out the wazoo. Over the distant far side of the space hung the biggest American flag Adam had ever seen.

The lobby was predictably lousy with tourists, foreign and domestic, MAGA-hatted but otherwise indifferently costumed, all of them taking selfies. Plus: dozens of uniformed military people, many of them in dress whites, many of them with their families. Tourists were usually invisible to Washingtonians, like the city's humidity, something you lived with and mostly ignored. Here the tourists seemed as much a reason for the place as the marks in a Trump casino. Everyone in the country were marks in a Trump casino.

Adam walked past them into the Benjamin Bar & Lounge, past the four gigantic TVs over the bar area. The place was hopping already, with lobbyists and apparatchiks in dark business suits and single-color power sheaths. The high-back bar stools were also covered in blue velvet. He left his name with the hostess and took a place at the far end of the lounge. In his Men's Wearhouse sports jacket, Adam probably looked more like a tourist than anyone who had business at the hotel.

He had checked a photo of Damon online so that he would recognize him. The *Next Deal* co-owner was young, thirty-two, according to Google. CalTech, Oxford, *and* the Stanford Graduate School of Business. He wasn't in the bar now. Adam had arrived uncharacteristically early. He hated that. The Uber had come too soon. This reminded him of the tweet thread's cryptic suggestions.

He took a seat and ordered a twenty-nine-dollar Scotch. He needed it.

Twitter raged. People were exaggerating the age difference between him and Valerie, even though his date of birth was available on Wikipedia and hers at the time of the Max episode had been reported in the initial *Politico* story. The twelve-year gap became sixteen. Twenty-five years. At a certain point Valerie was going to have been in grade school. Now people wanted to know exactly what had happened that wasn't so glorious.

As if he hadn't thought of it once in twenty years, Adam revisited the proceedings in the Chi-Chi's single-occupancy public restroom, the shock of light, the tarnishing porcelain on the side of the urinal, the kidney shape of the gum in the urinal, the feel of the hairs on the backs of her legs on his lips, the blinding desire, his insistence, her resistance, his culminating incompetence. Many regrets had accrued. My God, this had happened on the occasion of her first and only magazine cover story.

And then @wtrapped came alive again.

Vainglorious male heterosexuality. The strutting. The conceit. The clumsy, adolescent wooing. The clumsy, adolescent, lame, useless lovemaking. Men get away with this all the time—because they hold power over us.

Meanwhile, it was already twenty past. No one in the bar looked plausibly like Damon. Adam had positioned himself in a visible place. He was assuming the unavoidably subordinate posture of someone waiting for someone else. He was almost done with his drink. Just in case, Adam texted the quant to let him know he was there, in the bar, sitting at the far end of the lounge.

Damon texted back several minutes later.

K

K? Now Adam was irritated. He was doing the guy a favor. He had dropped what he was doing to meet him (admittedly, on a day that was otherwise shot, what an understatement). He had come to this place for the good of an institution that he no longer had a connection with. He had come because he *believed* in the *Next Deal*'s mission. The right new editor for the magazine would set the progressive agenda for the post-Trump era. Adam believed there would be a post-Trump era. But if he was going to get *K*'d, fuck it.

And now, here it was, popping up on his phone, the email from Nuri Gelman at MSNBC that he had been waiting for.

The first augury was the absence of a subject line. He opened the email.

The letter was just three or four sentences, but he couldn't read them, for a kind of shroud had passed before his eyes, accompanied by a sharp pain behind them. Before the figurative darkness fell he glimpsed that he was being addressed as Adam Zweig, not Adam, and that the rest of the email was officious, boilerplate, impersonal, terse. Nuri was a close friend, going back more than a decade. She had brought him to the network originally. She had been the one to lobby for giving him a more regular on-air position. She had taken him out for a drink when the offer was made, and it could not be said, at the Del Frisco's bar, that there was no giddy, giggling, conceivably flirtatious subtext. The phone now literally went dark, to conserve the battery.

The contract was being withdrawn, obviously. Adam had been worrying about it, he knew the peril was out there, but he still hadn't expected it to happen, not over the fallout from events that occurred twenty years ago.

Now his other fears about not writing for the *Next Deal*, the *Guardian*, and other publications became more concrete. He considered each of the editors he worked with: every one of them a coward, or at least none of them valued him enough to fight to keep him in their pages in the face of public opprobrium. Not that these publications paid well. Not that these publications had raised their rates in a long time. He had really been counting on the money from MSNBC.

And for at least thirty years Adam had been confident of his easy access to print, sure that his reporting and his views mattered, that the words he was assembling on his desktop would shortly be read by an interested public. He could always call up an editor at the *New Yorker*, the *New York Times Magazine*, the *Next Deal*, or the *New York Review of Books*—he had all their numbers, their personal email addresses, and knew the names of their kids—and say he had something for them. Maybe they would take the story or some other editor would. And then the story would go into print or up on the web with his byline. He had taken for granted that he would always have a byline. That he would always have readers. Fuck, by the time @wtrapped was done with him, he wouldn't be getting a byline in the *Pennysaver*.

Adam had never really taken "cancel culture" seriously. Cancel culture was a right-wing bugbear, fabulated to defend bigoted speech and hateful behavior. The term's catchy alliteration apparently made it credible to susceptible minds. Adam had scoffed. He believed that certain expressions of hatred and certain misconduct should indeed lay beyond social acceptability. He was glad, for example, that there was a social cost to be paid by someone calling him a kike, even if the speech was legally protected by the Constitution. Certain actions that targeted individuals because of their social identities (whether they were based on race, sex, or something else) deserved ostracization or more. These actions included sexual harassment. Certain outrages warranted the forfeit of livelihood. Sure, fire the motherfucker who calls him a kike. Fire the other motherfucker who goes on air to deny the Holocaust.

He didn't think he was being hypocritical in seeing injustice now that cancellation was coming for him. He had already recognized that progressive manners of the day failed to discriminate between the range of possible misconduct and the range of sanctions. Judging every aspect of the situation with Valerie, every nuance that wasn't public, every nuance that was private to him only—notably the indelible recollection of the first warm touch of her hand on his, the squeeze—he didn't think he *deserved* cancellation. Even if the bald facts of the case suggested that his offense was greater, he didn't think he deserved to be punished *at the same time* as Max. They had committed very different offenses in different circumstances. But being that they were committed against the same serially mistreated woman, the two men would now be forever yoked to the same stocks in the same market square.

He felt the unfairness with an exquisite keenness, or rather as a dull, immobilizing weight. The weight seemed to flatten whatever it was that had ever existed between him and Valerie.

Not for the first time, but with unprecedented vigor, Adam was struck by the immensity of his own mortality. He had always identified as a journalist. He was a man who reported and a man who wrote. Now, if he couldn't get into print . . . Grief deepened into despair. He was then consumed by a flaming anger, the anger that rises within us all when we contemplate oblivion.

He saw himself from a distance, sitting alone in this sleazoid Trump bar, nearly through his Scotch, which may have well been watered down per corporate policy, watching himself getting reviled and laughed at on social media. He imagined that if social media could see him at this moment, he would look even more pathetic. The next tweet from @wtrapped would raise his pitifulness by several orders of magnitude. He straightened his sport jacket. A waitress asked him if he'd like something else. He said he was still waiting for someone. He heard himself sound a little forlorn. He listlessly observed the waitress's short, tight skirt. Its brevity and constraint were matched by the suits worn by the women in the lobby on business. Everyone seemed corseted, pushed-up, overpainted, and overperfumed. There was enough blondage milling around the bar to staff a Viking longship or a Fox News midday program. Whose ideal of women was this? The women at the Trump bar left him so cold, so close to absolute zero, that Adam wondered whether he had ever cared for women at all. He wondered if his lifelong pursuit of the opposite sex had been pointless and degrading, simply something mindlessly purchased at great cost from the rotten men-owned, women-selling society in which he lived. And there was more degradation to come.

Still no Damon Brosseau.

He stared at his notifications—they were coming in hard. Twitter (or at least the nanoscopic subset of it that cared) had reached a consensus that more information was required to understand what had been "clumsy, adolescent, lame, useless" or, as it was now termed, #CALU. The idea of it was apparently hilarious, at least in regard to him. And shameful. They were waiting for @wtrapped to post again.

He touched the compose icon, not entirely idly.

It's all true.

He touched the Post button, again not entirely idly.

He refreshed his feed. His tweet was there at the top, in his name, alongside the tightly cropped headshot from 2013. He was frightened to see it there. He was also thrilled, as if this were his first time in print. He felt the surges of pride and power that, he knew, accompanied actions of great recklessness. It already had three likes.

He self-replied: *It's true. There's more to be known, if anyone's interested.*

That's right. There was plenty of *TK* where that came from.

If anyone's interested: love in the afternoon, after deadline. Also in the morning. Also at night, when we could get away together. Some of these mornings, afternoons, and nights followed one another within a single diurnal period, leaving us spent, yet impatient for the dawn. . . .

If anyone had observed him at the bar, they would have thought he was grinning like an idiot.

Weekend getaways to Blue Ridge and the Eastern Shore. Memorable lovemaking at the Annapolis Inn and a cabin in the Poconos, and not only under the sheets. Also on a hilltop in Theodore Roosevelt Park. In a canoe.

That sounded dangerous.

Gentlemen should be discrete, especially about their romantic exploits. I can confirm only that I would never again feel myself so physically alive, so physically present. Nor so capable.

Ha ha!

And in these latter years I warmly recall the pleasures taken by my partner so long ago, her avidities, her happy little gasps and cries, not to mention the invention she brought to the tasks at hand.

Five days in Cancun . . . I hear there's a beach there.

Adam loved saying *Cancun* to himself, for its internal rhyme.

Affection, sympathy, exploration, need, passion.

He paused here, to let a wave of feeling shudder through him.

Were we each carried forward by desire? Did we each believe we were free, longing, self-controlling individuals? I thought so. I wasn't considering power relations. I can say only that human tenderness, human comfort, and the human kiss possess their own moral values.

"Mr. Zweig?"

It took a moment for Adam to lift his head out of Twitterspace.

His name had been pronounced by a woman of beauty and elegance and bright wide eyes, finely sculpted features, pillowy lips, and translucent skin. She was slightly stooped in front of his table, her décolletage in his face. At first he thought it was some angel or houri trying to disprove his avowal of disinterest, and it almost worked, and then he recognized her as the bar hostess.

He muttered something in assent.

She stepped aside, revealing that her shapely form had somehow eclipsed a diminutive-ish young man in a white panama hat hovering in the space behind her.

This was Damon Brosseau? This kid in a pale blue linen guayabera? He looked at least ten years younger than thirty-two, more like a college student on spring break. It was a classic guayabera, untucked with four wide pockets in the front, like straight from Kingston.

Adam observed that the lower left pocket was stuffed with papers, perhaps tourist brochures and travel receipts. This kind of ruined the effect. His upper right pocket held a hotel key card. He was just a tourist kid.

"Yo," Damon said heartily, or perhaps it was no more than an attempt to sound hearty.

The young man lowered himself into the chair across from Adam and grinned at the spectacle around them. He didn't seem to be aware that he was a half hour late. He was still processing the scene.

Adam's phone now exploded like a car bomb. He nonchalantly powered it off.

Adam said, for want of anything else, "Welcome to Trumpville."

"It's wild."

Adam wondered exactly what Damon found wild. Did they not have fancy-tacky hotels in Jamaica? Was it the gilt? The swarm of lobbyists? With their professional association lapel pins? The aroma of blowtorched candied bacon, a specialty of the house? Steve Mnuchin, at a table in the other corner of the lounge, squinting at his phone, too vain to wear reading glasses?

When the waitress came over, Damon stared in frank appreciation. Adam thought the boy was more impressed than he should have been. Damon ordered a Coke.

Adam tried to begin the conversation by asking him whether it was his first time in town. Damon said that the partners had come when they bought the magazine. He didn't elaborate. Adam realized that he didn't know how to. As Adam had discovered years ago when he did the interview, the quant could make an effort to be open and friendly, at least about things he cared about, but he labored with small talk. Adam wondered whether he should ask him about Jamaica or how he got involved with quantitative analysis. Instead he asked about his fantasy baseball team.

"Yeah, we're doing pretty well this year," Damon said, happy to speak of it. "Charlie Morton, J. T. Realmuto. I told you we have Bellinger."

Adam reminded himself that this was *fantasy* baseball, not the game of baseball, which, like any game, was a kind of a fantasy in itself—so, a fantasy of a fantasy. Politics, at least, was a fantasy about a real thing, a game being played whose end results held sway upon the lives of real men and women.

Meanwhile, in another fantasy universe, on a rocky, Earth-sized, habitable-zone exoplanet, dramatic, catastrophic events were taking place. Adam's name was being spoken over and over, in an insistent angry roar. And a surprised roar: he had confirmed a romantic affair! You rarely ever got that. But had he really confirmed one? Adam's tweets were generating storms of confusion. With the phone off, however, this planet and its weather were as notional as Damon's baseball team.

"That's great," Adam said, reminding himself again of the other world's absence. "So, as I mentioned, I have some thoughts about the next editor."

"Yeah," Damon said, shaking his head. "What a problem. I still don't understand how something like this could have happened."

"Sure, but now you've got to look ahead, you've got to think about the future of the magazine. It still has an influential readership. The Democrats have to develop strong, persuasive positions in the next few months. On climate change, China, Iran . . . The list is formidable."

"Yeah," Damon said. "You know, Silas is the one who really cares about politics. He reads every issue. He was the one who wanted to buy the magazine. Because of Max."

Adam said agreeably, "Max was universally admired. I'm sure the situation is upsetting for you both."

Damon shrugged. "Silas is totally doing his weed thing right now. Prop 2 in Utah. Prop 64 in California. Prop 537 in American Samoa. He's always flying off somewhere. If he's not already high."

Adam discerned resentment.

"But he agreed that Max had to resign?"

"I guess," Damon said. "He's a hard guy to reach these days. It was really my girlfriend who said he had to go. She's the associate publisher, you know. She said he had become a huge liability. She's on Facebook, Twitter, Instagram, whatever. She's involved like you wouldn't believe. She's always looking at her phone. You can't talk to her when she's looking at her phone. I tell you, though, for Max to lose his job over this is cray cray."

Adam wondered what was being said about him on Instagram. He had forgotten about Instagram. He should look. He wondered also how it was that they had made Damon's girlfriend the associate publisher. Was she qualified? Not that he was sure what an associate publisher did or how qualified she had to be. But the third wonderment now was the implication that Damon Brosseau, a guy whose technical innovations had revolutionized the financial industry, didn't engage in social media. He was hardly aware of it. How was that possible? Was there a profound secret being revealed here? Adam should listen closely. Did the real masters of digital technology, the ones who harvested profits from our slavish unpaid screen tappings, know that social media was for chumps?

"Right," Adam said. Had Damon talked to anyone but his girlfriend? Did he have a staff monitoring public opinion? No, his business didn't depend on public opinion. Costs and benefits were determined by financial indicators, terms of mystery like price-earnings ratios, discounted cash flows, and option pricing. A goofy kid still a-goggle at the Trump ambient excess, Damon nonetheless remained a quant dude. Adam added, "Yeah, it's a shame."

Damon grinned again, amazed. "And you're involved, too, right? You knew about the pass!"

Adam said, "There have actually been some further developments. . . ."

"My girlfriend thought it was nuts for me to even meet you. That it would look bad if anyone saw us."

Someone could conceivably identify Adam here. But they wouldn't recognize with whom he was meeting. Adam said, "I think you're safe."

"Yeah, that was just her opinion. *You* were quoted in the *New York Times*."

Adam tried to redirect the conversation.

"I think I've come up with two excellent candidates," he said, still unsure which of the two women deserved the stronger recommendation. He was waiting to see how the conversation went. He needed to figure out how radical a departure Damon wanted for the publication.

"I mean, Max once made a pass? You know how many passes I've made? Sometimes they're successful, sometimes you get shot down. My girlfriend didn't say yes right away. But I was mucho attracted. She's super-smart, has a great personality, very fit, used to be a Pilates instructor. The first time I asked her out she refused, but I was persistent. I kept on going over to her desk. I kept on asking what she was doing for lunch. Finally she gave in. It helped that I was her boss. So things worked out. And now she's the associate publisher. Part-time. She's also in systems."

Adam smiled weakly.

"That's lovely," he said. "I'm not saying what happened with Max is fair, but we have to recognize that this is the moment we live in. And, to stay relevant, the *Next Deal* has to be part of that moment."

Adam began by offering Charlotte Skinner, a name that Damon didn't recognize, even though she had written several important, news-making pieces for the *Next Deal* during his tenure as co-owner. Adam emphasized her reputation and experience. He also repeated a well-worn anecdote about the time she cornered Ari Fleischer in the White House men's room, at the urinal, and also the story about her running across the minefield during the First Chechen War. It occurred to Adam that this was a war Damon might not have heard of. Nor the Second. Adam could see that he was losing Damon's attention. It had wandered away to the scene at another table, where a tuxedoed waiter was about to open a bottle of champagne with a fucking saber.

It was a tourist thing, performed for a middle-aged couple in drawstring slacks. The waiter removed the foil from the bottle, leaving the wire cage still attached to the cork. He flourished the Trump Winery–branded tool, which was about eight inches long. He took a few practice strokes, dramatically running the blade against the bottle's seam. Everyone was watching now. In a single quick motion the blade screeched up the bottle and the neck, removing the cork and the top of the bottle itself. The pop was heard across the bar and someone lost an eye. There was scattered applause. The practice was called sabrage.

"Charlotte's just one candidate," Adam said, once the tourists' glasses were filled and Damon had turned back to him. "I'll send you her contact info. The other person I was thinking of is Kristina Newhouse. I don't know her well, but she's a historian and a forceful writer. She wrote a terrific book about Northern slavery. I can send you the pieces she's done for the *Post*. She has interesting, original perspectives on income inequality, gay rights, and structural racism, and how these issues can involve one another."

Damon was still impressed by the saber, but this seemed to have caught at least some of his interest.

"What is she, Black?"

Adam was startled by the directness of the question.

"Yes," he said, with careful indifference.

"Cool," Damon said. "Would that be, like, a big deal?"

"She would bring something new to the magazine," Adam said carefully. "I think she'd have ideas about invigorating the coverage, to make it more reflective of contemporary thought. And she might be able to reach a younger, edgier audience. I'll send you both her and Charlotte Skinner's information. And, if you'd like, I can reach out to either of them myself, to see if they're interested. I don't mind doing the introductions."

Damon appeared to consider the offer, an act of generosity that Adam had not expected to make. But now Adam didn't think the kid had the capability or inclination to contact the women on his own. Adam wondered who else Damon would ask for advice, if anyone else was going to help him right the ship. Whether he cared if the ship sank. A sunk ship would be yet another tax write-off.

But now some kind of transformation seemed to be working itself upon Damon's boyish features. They turned into something no longer boyish. It was startling to watch. The alterations were nearly total. Brow furrowed, jaw set, Damon looked away with an intense gaze that might have been contemplating the magazine's leadership decision, or some complicated computational problem, or the mechanics of the cork removal that he had just witnessed. He was submerging into himself, into his mind's oceanic depths. Adam wondered how much of what he told him the co-owner had absorbed.

Damon forced himself to return to the conversation. "Which *Post* does she write for?"

"*Washington*," Adam said, stifling a gasp.

Now that Adam had made the stronger case for Kristina Newhouse, he thought Skinner was the better candidate. Max should have brought Newhouse in as a writer—he had

missed quite a few good hires—but the day-to-day operations needed someone with magazine experience. Charlotte
would slide into the position most easily.

"I know Bezos," Damon distantly murmured to
himself.

"You'd like me to put you in touch with them?"

"Sure," Damon said carelessly. The carelessness
was unfeigned. His preoccupation with whatever he
preferred to think about had drained whatever reserves
of bonhomie he had brought into the bar. "Why not?"

"Both? Do you want me to talk to both of them?"

"I guess," he said.

Adam now observed a significant tremor of restlessness cross Damon's face. It was triggered by Adam's
attempt to confirm whom he should call. Damon was
suddenly impatient with the conversation. Nevertheless,
Adam thought, this talk about the future of the *Next
Deal* was important enough to demand the dude's full
consideration. Fuck him. Adam was just doing him a
favor, he reminded himself. Let him get irritated.

"Kristina teaches at Brown University in Providence,
Rhode Island," Adam said very slowly, deliberately
drawing it out to annoy Damon further. "The Watson
Institute for International and Public Affairs. The
semester's probably done so she might be traveling. She
gives lectures all over the world. Jakarta. Reykjavík.
Ouagadougou. But why don't I set up a telephone conversation first? Then, depending on how it goes, you

can make arrangements to meet each other. Here or in Providence. Charlotte Skinner's in Washington, so I think probably more easily available. She's the national security correspondent for the *Daily Beast*."

"Why don't you do it?""

"Yeah, glad to," Adam said curtly. "As soon as I return to my office."

"No, I mean run the magazine."

Damon didn't seem to be joking. The restlessness on his face was still etched there. Adam understood that he had very little capacity for boredom; maybe that was what made him a quant dude, some kind of not-very-interesting genius: his focus on only what he found mentally stimulating, down to its smallest intricacies, and his compulsive appetite for stimulation. And everything about Washington declined to stimulate him: the monumental architecture, the superblocks, the office workers defined by GS grade, the politics. The bar at the Trump Hotel was the most compelling thing in the nation's capital so far. And the most compelling thing in the bar, except maybe the waitress, had been the opening of the champagne bottle. Now that was over. Adam wondered if politics had become even less compelling for him since he and Silas bought the *Next Deal*. Silas really should have been the one to come to Washington.

Adam didn't allow himself to take the proposal seriously, not yet. He wasn't sure that this wasn't some kind of game Damon was playing, for some recondite entertainment. Adam became aware again of the lobbyists around them, the businessmen and the congressional staffers, the low urgent hum, the occasional humorless laugh. The other men in the Trump bar were playing games, some unrelated to either business or politics. Some of it was simply personal one-upmanship, a strategy to expose the other guy. This is what guys did. But, Adam intuited, this wasn't the kind of game Damon liked to play. For him human behavior wouldn't be sufficiently interesting.

Adam went back to studying the young man, who still seemed annoyed. He had stopped staring at the sights around the lobby at least. He was waiting for an answer, increasingly peeved. Adam no longer thought of him as a goof or a college kid, even with the hat and the guayabera.

Finally, Adam said, "That's the worst goddamn idea I ever heard."

Damon frowned.

"Are you interested in the job?"

"Are you paying attention? I'm deeply implicated in this whole business. I'm like public enemy number two. Look at Twitter."

Now Damon's face was visited by a shiver of contempt. "Twitter. Twitter's not the whole world, you know. Let's keep things in perspective. The main thing is that I need an editor for the magazine."

Adam didn't like being told that *he* was the one who was social media delusional.

He said, "Anyway, I think you're better off hiring a woman."

Damon was puzzled. "A woman?"

The quant dude, bless him, hadn't understood why the two candidates Adam had proposed were women.

"That's what people are expecting. After a sexual harassment situation."

Adam was aware that he could have made a fuller argument for a woman editor. He had just begun to think that Damon might be in earnest.

Damon said, "You don't want the job? You know something about the magazine, right? The *Times* said you used to work there."

"Thank you, I'm flattered you asked," Adam said, now letting the proposition sink in. He immediately thought of public policy issues that were getting insufficient attention. He thought of some immediately assignable stories. The magazine's design needed to be refreshed too. And then he thought of the names of the journalists that Max had dangled in front of him this morning, all slightly more illustrious than Adam's. Not any longer. Once more a door opened. He still wasn't sure that Damon was for real. "But if I come in, don't you see how this is going to blow up? You should talk to your girlfriend first."

"My girlfriend doesn't run my business," Damon said.

"Well, she made the announcement about Max."

"My girlfriend is a wonderful person," he said grimly. "But this kind of decision belongs to the principals."

There had evidently been an argument.

"Well, how about Silas?"

"Silas," Damon said, and Adam saw something like hurt in the co-owner's face. Or anger. That resentment again, possibly about his partner's dedication to nonbusiness matters. Adam wondered if the real reason they had moved their company to Jamaica was the ganja. Silas's idea. Damon made a small motion with his hand, waving the other people away with a little less indifference than he was attempting. He said, "Are you afraid?"

"No, of course not," Adam said, because what else could he say? What could he say about the Twitter salvo that had just been fired into the void? "People are going to claim you're rewarding me for my silence, for what they'll call my complicity. You're going to get blowback."

"So what? It's not like anyone's accusing you of sexual harassment," Damon said, rising from his chair while simultaneously tapping at his phone. With the decision made, the task completed, his face had relaxed again. He was back on spring break, determined not to let Washington, DC, get him bored again. The shirt really suited him, or would have if he took the crap out of the pockets. Adam wondered whether his girlfriend had picked it out. Damon added, "Anyway, I have to go. I have a timed ticket for the Spy Museum."

"I'm surprised you're not going to the Nats game. They're playing Arizona."

Damon shook his head. "I can't watch baseball. Too slow," he said. "Let's close this thing now. My office is sending you a contract."

ADAM KEPT his phone off. His house was dark when he arrived. Upstairs, he gently inserted himself into his office chair. He took pleasure in its ergonomic welcome home. He rolled back for the ride and stopped. He absorbed the quiet. He felt it seep down inside.

He slowly opened his devices. One by one, they began demanding his attention. They were shouting at him, with great insistence and at great volume. Disbelief at his tweet thread. Also belief. Derision. Fury. Attempts to survey the alpine heights of his assholery. Or rather its abyssal depths. There were some cute dancers on TikTok, apparently doing something interpretive.

The belief and the disbelief: some people were taking at least some of Adam's tweets as the literal truth, if not all of them, unsure how many to accept. They were going to great lengths to parse what *really* happened between him and Valerie. The derision: among these tweeters, he was being castigated for being so apparently boastful about his sexual adventures. The rage: for being so apparently candid about a private romantic episode. Not everyone fell for the tweet thread, of course. He was denounced for being a liar, the offense compounded

by the thread's intimacy. One pedantic troll came to
Adam's defense by observing that all of literature's great
lovers, like the Chevalier de Seingalt, otherwise known
as Giacomo Casanova, were liars.

But there was nothing from @viovine or @wtrapped.
There was nothing from Valerie at all.

Like the rest of Twitter, Adam waited for her
response. As a river of shit emptied into his feed during
the next hour, Adam had plenty of opportunity to
reflect, and not for the first time today, on his capacity
for personal sabotage. What an idiot he was. If he had
shown only the smallest iota of self-restraint . . . The
tweet thread, which had given him so much pleasure to
write, was perhaps the single most stupid thing he had
ever done. Even stupider than what he had done in the
Chi-Chi's restroom.

But as Valerie's silence extended, as she delayed
denying the veracity of Adam's account of their romance,
as she delayed declaring the *preposterousness* of Adam's
account of their romance, as Adam's series of tweets
was retweeted exponentially, Adam's account of their
romance took on a kind of factual solidity, at least on
Twitter, as things did on Twitter.

Adam imagined her anger rising and building. He
imagined it as a thunderhead looming over social media's
barren plains. Yet no word arrived from either account.
No gigajoule electrostatic discharge. No pressure-
induced sonic shock wave.

Maybe there wouldn't be. After all, Adam reflected, he had seemed to *confirm* that there had been sex. She would gain nothing by contradicting him about the particulars. It was even possible that her contradiction or refutation or clarification would only muddy the waters. It could even raise questions about what had happened in Max's office.

And here is the magazine contract. It's at the top of Adam's inbox, almost glowing in boldface. He wondered what Damon's girlfriend was saying to him, and at what amplitude and in what tone of voice. But Damon, in the museum now and surrounded by pigeon cameras, Enigma machines, shoes with hidden microphones, an Aston Martin DB5, and the axe used to kill Trotsky, might be saying I did what you asked me to do, and I had to take a plane to Washington to do it, so leave me the hell alone. Adam didn't know what Damon's relationship was like with the associate publisher who was a former Pilates instructor and hadn't wanted to go to lunch with him. Silas's anger might be roused, too, depending on what time it was in American Samoa.

Christ, they were giving him his own shitload of money. Adam signed the form right away and sent it back.

Aurelie Dumesnil called a moment later. "What the fuck, Adam?"

He had yet to meet Aurelie Dumesnil, but her pronunciation of the word *fuck* sent a shiver through his loins. So that was still happening.

"Hi!"

"You lied to me," she declared, as if no one had ever lied to the *New York Times* before.

"I didn't think what happened between me and Valerie was 'untoward' or 'improper.' I certainly didn't see it as a 'campaign for sexual conquest.' Anyway, it was a personal matter. I had a right to keep that to myself."

"This whole issue is personal!" she exclaimed, exasperated. "That's why sexual harassment is so pernicious. It confuses a woman's most personal desires, her deepest intimacies, with the demands of her professional life, the work she does to earn her daily bread. Sexual harassment makes it impossible for this woman, any woman, to have a true personal self, to have the freedom to make her own romantic choices and to have agency over her own body. *Of course* it's personal. It's the way a patriarchal society corrupts the personal!"

"Well, anyway . . ."

"I'm going to have to ask you a direct question. Is your tweet thread admitting that you had an affair with Valerie Iovine?"

"Really, Aurelie."

"Did you have *sex* with Valerie Iovine? Yes or no."

He chuckled as if he were having a good time.

"Listen, Aurelie," he said. "I have a scoop for you!"

"C'mon, Adam, please answer my question."

"I've just been named editor in chief of the *Next Deal*."

There was no gasp or audible intake of breath, but

the silence was as deep as a winter night. He would have to wait it out.

Finally, she said, "They tell me, Adam, you used to have a reputation as a pretty good journalist. Now, I don't know what happened to you, but these statements . . ."

"Call them," he said. *A* pretty good *journalist?*

"You're not shitting me again?"

"I wasn't shitting you the first time. Call them. They'll confirm."

"I will!"

He wondered if they really would confirm. Minds could be changed. His mentions had gone through the roof, past the stratosphere, into the Van Allen belt. But if you didn't follow social media, the controversy would be something remote, second- or third- or fourthhand news, like the multifront war in the Congo, now in its twenty-third year. It was time to do a new article about that. He wondered who he could send.

He said, "But in the meanwhile, and you may want to quote me on this, I'm proud to be rejoining the team at the *Next Deal*, an institution with a storied history and a future vital to the preservation of American democracy. We'll continue to do great things at the magazine, setting a clear-headed, forward-thinking course for the next generation."

"I'm getting off the phone now. I'm calling them!"

And still there was no response from either @viovine or @wtrapped. Twitter demanded a response.

BUT VALERIE IOVINE was thinking of her capacity for
self-sabotage too. She was shocked that, starting with
her approach to the Washington news sites, she had put
herself in the middle of a #MeToo story. She had never
wanted to be part of *any* story; she too strongly identified
as a reporter. This was something Adam thought he knew
as true. The South Philly girl had always believed that
her job, only marginally white-collar, was nothing more
than to get the facts, build a narrative that made sense to
the reader, and file on time at the assigned length. That's
how she had done it at the *Yale Daily News*, that's how she
did it at the *Next Deal*, that's how she was doing it at the
Pilot. Confidently adversarial, reportorially aggressive,
well-spoken, quick-witted, and occasionally profane, she
was nevertheless self-conscious about drawing personal
attention: the only way that she could bear to raise her
hand at a press conference was by reminding herself that
she was doing it in service to the story.

Now, Adam imagined, she must have felt burned by
her moment of self-indulgence, by how she had allowed
herself to get sucked into the self-dramatizing whirlpool
of social media. She had been *tricked* by social media into
thinking that she wanted to be part of the story. She had
been tricked by #MeToo. The first regrets came when
she saw her name in the *Politico* piece. The Cut article
had been a deeply painful exercise, no matter how pre-
meditated her submission to the magazine. But she had
read or been told or had absorbed from popular opinion

that a personal narrative could be somehow liberating or empowering. The next regrets came when she hit Send Seeing it up on the site had been a mortification. This was the Age of Mortification. She cringed about what she had revealed of herself.

Now everyone was talking about her: her colleagues at the paper, her editors, her neighbors, people she had never met and didn't know, her name sullied upon their chapped, yapping lips. Her parents would find out about this public spectacle soon enough. So would Donna Franzoni. And then she had thought she had been clever about @wtrapped, as if she could really predict what would happen on social media. As if she made good judgments when she was angry. As if she was good at revenge. And now there was Adam's fucking tweet thread. News of that would eventually reach her parents too.

That fucker Adam. That fucker fucker fucker fucker Adam, Adam imagined.

And now? Now? Valerie read about his new appointment. She swore. Then she laughed, bitterly. Then she swore again, tears stinging. That prick had totally boxed her in. She was reminded, again, of the goddamn Chi-Chi's restroom.

THE *NEXT DEAL* was located in the same building where it had been when Adam worked there. He hadn't visited the office in years. The carpeting was new, he supposed, though he couldn't recall what the old carpeting had been like. He observed the same dropped ceilings and orange-fabric-lined cubicles from his time on staff. Personnel had cycled in and out with their things, so new photos were stuck to old bulletin boards and new sweaters were draped on the backs of old chairs in anticipation of the overpassionate summer air-conditioning. The coffee station had been moved to where the recently devalued copiers and dot matrix printers had been installed.

The morning was still early. He was the first to come in, after making arrangements with the staff IT guy last night. Adam had been up all night, planning, and also waiting for a revocation that never came.

Max had removed his most obviously personal knickknacks, like pictures of his wife and daughter, but he had left everything else that had accumulated during his decades of editorship, which was impossible to separate from his personal life. The bookshelves were packed, every space on top of the vertical books laid with the horizontal. The filing cabinets were still stuffed, sloppily, and several file folders were left out. There was a general, lived-in disorder to the office. Adam hadn't looked in the desk drawers yet.

OK, Adam would have to live with Max's mess for a while. That was an implicit part of the takeover. Once tempers cooled, hopefully in a few weeks, Adam would have to arrange to return most of the detritus. Perhaps he could conduct these negotiations with Max's wife, though he had no idea how she felt about the situation. She could be angry at Adam too. Or at Max, if the incident with Valerie was news to her. Or if it had resonances with the beginning of their own courtship. Or she could excuse Max *because* it had resonances with their own courtship. You never knew.

Meanwhile, Max had assigned pieces for the next several issues. He had also laid down procedures for editing and production. He had developed his own way of operating, and that would continue to define the magazine's protocols, giving it the momentum to keep publishing through the turmoil. Adam would have to inhabit Max's presence for some time, like sleeping in unchanged linens. That would be all right, he thought, a little creepy and also a little comfy.

As he waited for the staff to come in, Adam studied the story lineup for the next issue and the layouts that had been completed. Phil Musgrove had also written an Andrew Yang piece, but it wasn't as good as the one Adam did for the *Guardian*. Musgrove didn't really understand the ramifications of the monthly checks. It would be too late, and too impolitic, to ask for changes. Adam eventually heard the first staffers come in and get settled. People would come and go through the morning. He listened for what sounded like a critical mass. The arrivals were accompanied by a low, rustling, rancorous hum. They had seen the closed office door, not to mention their social media feeds.

At this moment his game face would have to comprise

a warmish smile that acknowledged the weight of recent events. Also: humility. This required several moments to assemble, his hand resting on the doorknob.

He eventually opened the door. When he did, he submitted to a moment of vertigo, seeing the outer office as Max always had. Two or three people had already come forward. He slowly took the place in the room where Max had always addressed the staff, in front of the three rows of cubicles. The buzz went silent, like a hive wiped out by climate-induced colony collapse.

"Hey, everybody."

He waited and people unsteadily, with small steps, as if pushing against a current, made their way to the front of the office. The personnel had changed over several times since he had been on staff, but he knew most of the eight or nine writers and editors who were there, either from freelancing for the magazine or from other gigs. He was less familiar with the production people. Everybody, of course, had heard the news. It was all they could think about.

"Hi," he began.

The faces were not what you'd call expectant. Or hopeful. The expressions on the faces of his new employees, men and women, were mostly resentful, or cold, or simply stunned. It was as if the whole of Twitter was in front of him, glaring. The difference with Twitter was that everyone was speechless.

Adam offered a few words of introduction. He said

he was pleased to be there. He reminded them that, besides being a former staff writer, he had contributed to the magazine for more than twenty years. He had then planned to acknowledge that the events surrounding Max's dismissal had been disturbing. He had planned on saying a lot more, especially about reaffirming humanist ideals in the pages of the *Next Deal*, but the audience didn't encourage him to go on. He stopped. He grinned at the rushing, rising swell of the staff's hostility. He finally, simply, said, "OK, let's put out a magazine."

He returned to his office and shut the door, listening to the resurgence of mutters, murmurs, and whispers. He heard the forging of resolve. He wondered how many resignations there would be. A few. A magazine staff position was an excellent job, relatively well paying and prestigious, but magazine journalists were accustomed to resigning, especially in anger. You might even call them a resigning class. That was OK. He'd hate to lose Sibila Fiore, the business and economics writer, the only one on the staff who understood money, which was kind of pathetic, but the others could mostly be replaced.

Regardless of who might leave, Adam had already decided on his first email of the morning, before he even spoke to the chief designer about the schedule for the rest of the issue's pages. He needed several minutes to write the note.

He wouldn't offer Kristina Newhouse a staff position

right away. He didn't think she would leave Brown for an ordinary magazine job. But he would say he'd love to have her on the masthead as a contributing editor. He wouldn't name a figure, not yet. And if Kristina Newhouse *did* want to leave academia, because it was so boring and inconsequential, Adam would put her on staff in a heartbeat. She could stay in Providence.

He'd get Skinner back too.

The designer came into his office on her own, as sullen as the rest of them, but with a problem that was apparently urgent. The Yang jump ran short, leaving a few inches of white space at the bottom of page 44. The hole was too small for art. Adam shrugged and said put in a house ad. She nodded and left and Adam realized that this was something that Max would have needed to sign off on. He marveled that he was now the one to do it.

After she left, Adam turned to an email that had arrived late last night, with a series of pdfs attached. The subject and message fields had been left blank. The pdfs comprised a two-page résumé and a half dozen newspaper feature articles on diverse subjects: overfishing on the Chesapeake, affordable housing in Newport News, etc.

Adam had immediately gone over every one of the pieces from top to bottom, the overfishing story for the second time. As local newspaper feature articles, they were well done, arguably better than well done. Solid reporting, as always.

Let Adam read what he liked into the absence of a

cover letter. That was the idea. Adam would be allowed
to think she was making a demand to be hired, to buy her
silence about what had really happened between them.
Or asking for a job as compensation for what had really
happened between them. Or the email may have been no
more than a simple job application to someone who once
knew her and had been familiar with her work, a request
to consider her education, her employment history, and
her best clips, as purposeful and aspirational and honest
and dishonest as any job application. The ambiguity was
the message itself. Not that she wasn't still pissed off.

He imagined her coming into the office, occupying
one of the cubicles, shuffling between the desks, arriving at staff meetings. He would know she was there, on
the other side of his office wall. He'd wait for her copy to
come in. She would be an enduringly conspicuous presence at the magazine. He might assign her to write on
workplace sex issues. Her return to the *Next Deal* would
be a story for a few days, she would suffer that. Columns
would be written either about the justice of the hiring
or its cynicism, and maybe it would take some heat off
him, except for those die-hard tweeters who would say it
would *never* take the heat off him. They would say they
could see through him all the way.

He and Valerie would never speak about what had
happened in the single-occupancy public restroom outside the doors to the Chi-Chi's restaurant. The recollection of what happened would be like a pebble in his shoe,

an irritant that he would allow as almost welcome. Let it blister. Let it suppurate. Let it stink. Something would remain between them in all its uncertainty, accompanying the other mysteries that permeated our lives.

He would write back in a few moments. Before that he gazed from the big window at the Capitol glistening under the morning sun and the cloudless blue sky. Things were happening in the city below. Bad things, mostly. Pompeo and Bolton were pushing for a military attack on Iran. Trump had announced the appointment of a new hardline "border czar," a former cop. The Capitol remained almost close enough to touch. Adam couldn't touch it, but hundreds of copies of the new *Next Deal* would be delivered there in a few days, his name at the top of the masthead. The building dominated the view from his new office and around it sprawled the rest of the fucked-up panorama, this city of misjudgment and ambition, of expediency and ideals, and of heartbreak and recovery, offering the possibility that there might yet be such a thing as human progress.

ACKNOWLEDGMENTS

The author thanks MacDowell for a productive and stimulating fellowship in the course of writing this novel. The author is also grateful for the generous support of La Maison Dora Maar and the Nancy B. Negley Artists Residency Program.

KEN KALFUS has been a finalist for the National Book Award and the PEN/Faulkner Award, and he has received a Pew Fellowship in the Arts and a fellowship from the John Simon Guggenheim Memorial Foundation. He is the author of five novels, including *2 A.M. in Little America* and *Equilateral*, and has published three short story collections. He has written for the *New York Times*, *Harper's*, the *New Yorker*, and the *New York Review of Books*. His books have been translated into more than ten languages. Born in New York, Kalfus currently lives in Philadelphia.

milkweed
EDITIONS

Founded as a nonprofit organization in 1980, Milkweed
Editions is an independent publisher. Our mission is to
identify, nurture, and publish transformative literature,
and build an engaged community around it.

We are based in Bdé Óta Othuŋwe (Minneapolis)
in Mní Sota Makhóčhe (Minnesota), the traditional
homeland of the Dakhóta and Anishinaabe (Ojibwe)
people and current home to many thousands of
Dakhóta, Ojibwe, and other Indigenous people,
including four federally recognized Dakhóta nations
and seven federally recognized Ojibwe nations.

We believe all flourishing is mutual, and we envision
a future in which all can thrive. Realizing such
a vision requires reflection on historical legacies
and engagement with current realities. We humbly
encourage readers to do the same.

milkweed.org

Milkweed Editions, an independent nonprofit literary publisher, gratefully acknowledges sustaining support from our board of directors, the McKnight Foundation, the National Endowment for the Arts, and many generous contributions from foundations, corporations, and thousands of individuals—our readers. This activity is made possible by the voters of Minnesota through a Minnesota State Arts Board Operating Support grant, thanks to a legislative appropriation from the Arts and Cultural Heritage Fund.

Interior design by Mike Corrao
Typeset in Bulmer

Bulmer was created in the late 1780s
or early 1790s. This late "transitional" typeface was
designed by William Martin for William Bulmer,
who ran the Shakespeare Press.